The engine died and the plane dropped

The crunching of metal onto the ground and trees came next. Natalie raced along the runway to the crash site, where the scene of twisted wreckage filled her with terror.

A movement claimed her attention. It was Colter straining to open the caved-in door. Sobs tore at her throat. Then her vision blurred as the shimmering haze burst into flames.

"Colter!" she screamed, her heart filled with terror that he would die. "Colter! No!"

In that frozen second of utter danger, Natalie knew she didn't want Colter to die, as she had often thought. She loved him! She wanted him to live!

JANET DAILEY

Fiesta San Antonio

Harlequin Books

TORONTO • NEW YORK • LONDON
AMSTERDAM • PARIS • SYDNEY • HAMBURG
STOCKHOLM • ATHENS • TOKYO • MILAN

This edition published July 1990
ISBN 0-373-83214-1

Harlequin Presents edition published June 1977
Janet Dailey Treasury edition 1985

Original hardcover edition published in 1977
by Mills & Boon Limited

CHAPTER ONE

THE BLACK velvet sky was studded with diamond stars, a cloudless Texas night, warm and languid. But there was a crackle of excitement in the air as the eyes of the crowd lining the banks of Paseo del Rio focused on the river parade.

A man stood in the crowd, but he was not a part of the festive throng. Tall, whipcord-lean, he stood aloof, expressing an aura of detachment. The cold, chiselled lines of the handsome face belonged to a man who rarely smiled, who had found no reason to smile for a long time.

Thick light-brown hair fell with careless attraction over his forehead, the slight waves streaked with burnished gold from long hours in the sun. The teak-dark tan of his complexion emphasised the impression that the face had been carved from wood, dispassionate and indifferent, without a soul. His eyes seemed to hesitate between green and blue, but there was always a frosty tint to their colour.

A gaily decorated barge floated under the stone footbridge, its bright lights blazing for the benefit of the crowd gathered along the river's bend at Arenson River Theatre. A murmur of appreciation rippled through the spectators. The young girl standing in front of the man glanced quickly at him, her blue eyes feverish with excitement.

"Look at that one, Daddy," she breathed in awe. "Isn't it beautiful?"

"Yes." There was a suggestion of an impatient sigh in his clipped agreement, but the girl's attention had returned to the parade.

His gaze flickered uninterestedly over the float and back to the child in front of him, a single, long brown braid nearly touching the waistband of her dress. How old was Missy? Colter Langston wondered idly, then silently cursed that he couldn't remember if his own daughter was ten or eleven.

He snapped a gold lighter to his cigarette, the brief flame throwing his arrogant features into sharp relief, inhaled deeply, then cupped the burning tip in his hand. What was he doing here? His eyes swept the crowd in contempt. People stood elbow to elbow, craning their necks for a glimpse of the floats when they could have remained at home and had an unobstructed view of the parade on their television sets.

"Observing the Fiesta is not participating." Unbidden Flo Donaldsen's statement came to him.

Yes, it was his aunt who was to blame for his presence in the crowd, his aunt and the prickles of conscience over the years of his neglect of Missy. Not neglect, Colter corrected silently. His daughter had never wanted for anything. She had beautiful clothes, plenty of food, a home. He had never sent her off to any boarding school. She had lived under the same roof with him since the day she had entered this world. What more could the child want from him? he thought impatiently.

This shy, quiet withdrawn child with her thin, sensitive face was his daughter. Yet Colter Langston felt no surge of emotion at the knowledge. He cared for her—as much as he could, but there was no bursting warmth of pride to fill the emptiness within him. With his usual cynicism, he decided that parenthood was vastly overrated.

Grinding out the half-smoked cigarette beneath the heel of his boot, Colter Langston glared resentfully at the slow-moving minute hand of his watch, knowing the parade had barely started and wishing it was over. There was an ominous tightening of his lean jaw as he realised he had committed himself to accompanying Missy to all the activities of Fiesta week, the celebration marking Texas's independence of Mexico. The River Parade was the first major event and he was already bored. Idleness didn't appeal to him.

With a self-mocking movement of his mouth, he admitted that there was little that didn't bore him. An only child, a son, born the heir to the vast Langston holdings in the Texas hill country north of San Antonio, he had been denied nothing as a child, a wild teenager, or a young man. Now, at thirty-four, he realised his senses were satiated. Life held no more illusions. Sex, love, marriage, all were coldly dismissed. The happiness and satisfaction that were supposed to exist in those items were the products of writers' and poets' imaginations. Colter had tried them all and found them wanting.

For the last five years, since his father's death, he had been the sole owner of the Langston Ranch and its numerous investments. The power of the Langston influence was his to command and he was accustomed to being obeyed.

Matt Langston had taught him that every man had a price, monetary or otherwise. Colter had admired and respected his father, but they had never been close. His mother had died when he was six and he had only photographs to recall what she looked like.

As for his wife Caroline, she had married the Langston name. It hadn't taken Colter long to realise that. The daughter she had died giving him within the first year of their marriage had been her means of cementing a permanent link with the Langston power and wealth. Her diary had callously stated that she had never loved Colter, only his money and name. Looking back, Colter realised that he had never loved her, only the perfection of her beauty. He had married her to satisfy the lust she aroused while adamantly withholding herself.

He had never loved anyone, not even himself. No one loved him. Missy tried, just as Colter had tried to love his father. Perhaps the one who came closest to caring for him had been his aunt Flo. When his mother had died, Matt Langston had brought her widowed sister to Langston Ranch to look after his son. She had stayed on to care for Missy.

But no longer. His mouth moved into a grim, forbidding line. At the end of this month, Flo Donaldsen was leaving, figuratively if not literally. She was a strong, proud woman who spoke her mind and Colter had received an unfaltering share of it before he and Missy had left for San Antonio.

"I don't like what you've become, Colter," she had told him. "You are cold, insensitive and sometimes cruel towards other people's feelings. You show more kindness and attention to your horses than you ever do to your own daughter, and it isn't right! You're cynical! Your heart has turned to stone—if you ever had one. Missy needs her father, not an ageing aunt. And if you can't be the parent she needs, then you should provide her with a mother. You'll not shirk your responsibility off on to me any longer. According to your father's will, the cottage by the creek is mine whenever I want it, along with a pension. I'll be moving into it at the end of the month."

Colter hadn't argued. Eventually he knew he could work his way around her. He had no qualms about using the affection she held for him and his daughter to gain what he wanted. Yet he had to admit that perhaps Missy deserved a mother.

Deirdre would relish the role. Granted he found her company to be stimulating and enjoyable, at least for the time being, but Colter knew that Deirdre only tolerated his daughter. The sensually attractive redhead was a man's woman, definitely not the domesticated type.

When the physical attraction Deirdre held for him passed, as it undoubtedly would—as it had with all the other women he had known—she would probably take her vengeance out on Missy. No, he would not marry Deirdre.

Candy tossed from a float landed at his feet, missing the outstretched hands that tried to intercept it. As Missy bent to retrieve it, a set of small fingers reached it first. A pair of dark brown eyes peered through the mop of thick brown hair falling over his forehead, their expression reluctant and hopeful.

"Was this yours?" The little boy's clenched fist opened to reveal the paper-wrapped candy, offering it hesitantly to Missy.

Colter watched the movement of his daughter's mouth into a refusing smile, noticing her lack of inhibition towards the child who was half her age.

"No, you can have it," Missy assured the little boy.

The tiny palm remained outstretched as the boy fixed his gaze longingly on the candy. "Nonnie said I wasn't supposed to take things that belonged to someone else, and I'm not supposed to take things away from girls."

Missy cast Colter a shy, adult smile before turning a solemn face back to the boy. "You found it, so you can keep it."

Bright brown eyes studied her face for an instant longer, then small fingers closed protectively over the candy. For precious seconds he held it in his fist before he reverently began unwrapping the paper.

"My name is Ricky," he said importantly after he had carefully placed the candy in his mouth. "What's yours?"

"My name is Missy and this is my father," she replied.

The boy named Ricky had to tilt his head way back to look up at Colter's face. One corner of Colter's mouth turned up in wry amusement at the open inspection he was receiving. He rather liked the boldness of the boy's look, forthright and not easily impressed. Nor intimidated, it seemed.

"I don't have a father," Ricky announced, "but some day I'm going to have cowboy boots, too."

The two thoughts did not correlate for Colter, but obviously they did for the boy. Briefly Colter wondered whether he and Missy would have been closer if she had been a boy instead of a girl. He doubted that. He would probably have been irritated by the constant demands of a son.

"Did your mother bring you to the parade?" Colter heard Missy ask.

He was a bit surprised at her interest in the boy. She had never seemed to display much interest in the other children she went to school with, although she had seemed fond of little Josh Harris. Still, Colter had presumed she was a loner like himself, the one trait they shared.

"Nonnie brought me," Ricky nodded, adding with a shrug, "but I think she got lost."

"Are you sure you're not the one who's lost?" Missy smiled.

"I don't think so." A small frown drew his brows together. "I know where I am, but I don't know where Nonnie is. So she's the one who's lost," he reasoned.

It was Colter's turn to frown as he saw his daughter touch the little boy's arm and bend slightly towards him in a solicitous movement.

"Yes, but you see, Ricky, your Nonnie knows where she is, but she doesn't know where you are. I'll bet she thinks you're the one who's lost," Missy explained.

The corners of his mouth pulled down. "I'll bet she'll be mad again," Ricky sighed.

"Where did you last see her?"

Colter guessed the trend his daughter's questions were taking and the last thing he wanted to do was become involved in a search for the boy's mother. If the boy was lost then it was his mother's fault for not keeping a closer eye on him.

"Over there somewhere." The boy's hand waved in the general direction of the foot-bridge. "I was thirsty and she was going to get me a drink."

"And you were supposed to wait for her," Missy concluded astutely.

More brown hair fell forward as the boy shamefacedly tucked his chin into his neck and answered a very small "yes."

"Give me your hand," Miss instructed quietly, "and we'll go and see if we can find her."

"Missy!" Colter's voice rang out sharper than he intended as his hand closed over her shoulder. He lowered his voice quickly to a firmer, less abrasive tone. "We are not going to search this crowd for the boy's mother," he said emphatically.

There was the hurt look of a wounded animal in her accusing eyes. "We can't just leave him. He's only a little boy, Daddy," she argued anxiously.

"I'm not so little," Ricky inserted proudly. "I'll soon be six."

Colter flashed him a silencing look of ice blue, then turned back to his daughter. She had withdrawn again into her shell, a remote resentment clouding her more calm blue eyes.

"Look," he sighed, his lips thinning with impatience at being backed into a corner. "We'll take the boy to that policeman over there. His mother has probably already discovered he's lost and will have notified them."

"Couldn't we take a few minutes to look first?" Missy suggested, glancing hesitantly at him through upcurving lashes.

"It isn't any of our business and we're not going to get involved," Colter snapped harshly.

His jaw tightened as Missy flinched from his tone. Fleetingly, he had to acknowledge that Flo was right when she said he hurt people without meaning to do it. Tact had never been one of his virtues. He abruptly released her shoulder and turned to the boy.

"Come on," he ordered crisply. "We'll take you to the policeman. He'll help you find your mother."

But Ricky held back. "They don't know where Nonnie is." His lower lip jutted out in a mutinous pout.

Colter stared at him for an instant, then reached down and swung the boy into his arms. Bright brown eyes curiously studied the face now at eye level. Unlike Missy, Ricky was not intimidated by the forbidding set of his jaw.

Nothing was revealed in Colter's expression, yet inwardly he admired the impertinent look.

The discovery had barely registered before the hint of green in his eyes returned to the cold, harsh blue. The child meant nothing to him. He pivoted sharply towards the distant man in police uniform, aware that Missy's feet were dragging as she followed him. As far as he was concerned it was enough that he had brought her to the Fiesta. It was ungrateful to involve him with this lost stray.

A small hand balanced itself on Colter's shoulder while Ricky took in his improved view of the crowd and the parade. Fingers tightened for a biting instant.

"Wait," Ricky ordered imperiously. His forefinger pointed to Colter's left. "There's Nonnie!"

Colter turned in the direction Ricky indicated, his alert gaze immediately picking out the woman frantically searching the crowd. As she drew nearer, a brow rose thoughtfully. Ricky's mother was hardly a woman. If Colter was any judge, she was barely out of her teens, and Ricky himself had asserted that he was almost six.

The girl was attractive, Colter decided, above average, despite the signs of exhaustion and strain etched in her features. The harried look had not occurred tonight but had accumulated over a period of months.

Then the hazel eyes, almond-shaped and slanted upwards at the corners, unusually attractive with their gold flecks, spied Ricky in Colter's arms. A wide smile of relief spread across her sensuously full lips as she hurried towards them. There was a vaguely untouched look about her that kindled a fleeting fire of desire in his loins until he remembered the boy in his arms. Women were available to him in abundance. He didn't need the entanglement of a small boy.

The crowds were so thick that Natalie was more terrified than she cared to acknowledge when she discovered Ricky was not where she had left him. He usually did exactly what he was told, although he might question the order. The excitement of the parade must have been too much for his adventurous nature to ignore.

Somehow she had known he wouldn't stray out of sight of the footbridge. Her fear had been that she would walk by him in the crowd and not see him. Only by the merest chance had she seen Ricky in the stranger's arms out of the corner of her eye.

"Oh, Ricky!" she exclaimed with a laughing cry as the stranger handed him to her, "I thought I told you to stay by the bridge."

Her relief at finding him unharmed was too great for Natalie to be as angry as she should have been with him. Tears filled her eyes, tears of relief and wretched tiredness. She brushed them away and proudly raised her head to thank the stranger.

Her breath caught in her throat, her body automatically stiffening at his bold appraisal of her slender form and the suggestion of jeering contempt. His aura of self-assurance bordered on arrogance. Natalie's initial impression had been that the man was handsome, but the unrelenting hardness of his face negated its effect.

The strange blue-green eyes seemed to strip away her pride. The expensive leisure suit of brown stitched with tan spoke of money and his gaze was too discerning not to recognise her clothes as bargain store purchases.

"I want to thank you for finding Ricky." Her expression of gratitude lacked sincerity, the result of his derisive look.

"You're holding me too tight," Ricky whispered loudly in her ear.

It was his way of saying that he was too big to be held like a baby in her arms. Reluctantly Natalie let him slide to the ground, keeping a firm hold of one small hand. Her shaking fingers clutched a paper cup in the other hand.

"He was no trouble." The low-pitched masculine voice drawled lazily, a contradiction to the alertness of his gaze. "We were taking him to the policeman on the corner."

Yes, Natalie thought with a kind of grim resentment, this arrogant stranger wasn't the type to involve himself more than superficially with the problem of a lost child, certainly not to the extent of participating in a search for her.

Ricky tugged at her hand. "They threw candy from the floats. I found a piece and Missy let me keep it. Was that all right? I've already eaten it," he added as an afterthought.

"Missy?" Natalie repeated blankly.

She followed his pointing finger, for the first time seeing the young girl standing beside the stranger. "That's Missy," Ricky explained, "and that's her father."

Compassion touched Natalie's heart. If the girl's father was as arrogant and callous as he looked, it was no wonder Missy seemed so sensitive and withdrawn. The girl was just reaching that awkward age when she needed the reassurance that somebody cared. Natalie remembered those heartbreaking years. If it hadn't been for her brother— But she had had her brother, and Natalie could only hope that the girl's mother was a vast improvement over her father.

"May I have my drink?" Ricky demanded.

"There isn't much left, I'm afraid," Natalie answered as she handed him the paper cup half-filled with water. "I spilled most of it looking for you."

He drained it dry and handed the empty cup back to her, wiping his mouth with the back of his hand. At that instant, Natalie noticed the marked silence of the stranger and realised he was probably very anxious for her to take Ricky and leave. Squaring her shoulders, she turned to him.

"Thank you again," she offered tautly. He nodded curtly in acknowledgement and Natalie tightened her hold on Ricky's hand. "Come on. Let's go watch the parade."

Her forced smile immediately changed into one of genuine loving at the sight of the bright brown eyes gazing back at her.

"Would you—" a hesitant voice began, stopping Natalie and Ricky as they began to turn away. "Would you like to watch the parade with us?" Missy faltered.

Natalie saw the sharp look of reproach that the man gave to his daughter and knew he wanted to be rid of them. She had guessed correctly. Gold fires flared for an instant in her eyes before she quickly banked them to meet the girl's wavering gaze.

"Thank you, but I don't think so," Natalie refused.

At the sideways look the girl gave her father, Natalie was aware that Missy had guessed the reason she had refused. There was a rebellious urge to stay just to spite the man, but Natalie knew she would be uncomfortable in his presence.

With more haste than was necessary she led Ricky through the crowds to the footbridge. Their previous vantage point near the river was occupied, much to Ricky's dismay. Natalie succeeded in finding a spot along the short, guarded rock wall where she could sit with Ricky perched on her lap. The minute she relaxed that aching tiredness swept over her, throbbing through every muscle and nerve.

The parade had started out as a treat for Ricky and a brief respite from her problems. It had barely begun when Ricky had become lost. What little energy she possessed had been expended in the search for him. She knew the stranger had silently condemned her for leaving the boy in the first place. Natalie acknowledged that he was partially right. But their vantage point for the parade had been such a good one and she had always been able to count on Ricky doing as he was told, so she hadn't dreamed he would stray from the spot. But what had gone right for her lately?

His small brown head leaned against her shoulder and Natalie rested her cheek against his silky fine hair. Her lashes fluttered tiredly down. If only she had someone to lean on, she sighed heavily. Her exhaustion was mental as well as physical. Sinking her teeth into the bottom of her lip, she tried to hold back the waves of despair.

That terrible weekend three years ago when her brother Ned and his wife had been killed outright in an automobile accident, then it had seemed so logical and natural for Natalie to take her little nephew Ricky to raise. It was either that or make him a ward of the courts to be placed in a foster home. At the time she had thought she had a good job. She couldn't have guessed that the firm would go out of business within a few months, nor did she realise the constant expense of a small child.

As the clothes, medical, and baby-sitter costs mounted, Natalie was forced to take nearly any kind of work to try to make ends meet. The last job she had worked through an agency that provided daily help to homes in the area. On Friday they had fired her when she was falsely accused of stealing from one of the homes. Her weekly pay check, no matter how frugally she spent it, had never succeeded in lasting till the next one. The few groceries in their tiny apartment would last out the week and no longer. She simply had to find another job soon.

The weight of the small boy on her lap seemed to increase, numbing her legs into leaden sticks. When the last float emerged from under the footbridge, Natalie realised that Ricky had fallen asleep. As she smoothed the straight brown hair from his forehead, she knew all her efforts had been worth it, and all the future ones, too. Ricky was strong and healthy, intelligent and happy, trusting and loving, and supremely confident that she loved him. There was no hint of the shyness, unhappiness, or uncertainty in Ricky that she had seen in Missy.

Gently Natalie turned Ricky into her arms, his hands automatically circling her neck in sleep and hugging her tightly. There was a warm sensation of love in the way the small body clung to her. Rising to her feet and carrying the heavy burden of the sleeping child that strangely felt lighter, Natalie followed the milling crowd that had begun to leave the riverwalk area.

The street leading to their apartment was much travelled and well lighted, one of the main thoroughfares to downtown San Antonio. As Natalie walked past the parking lot congested with cars attempting to leave, she wished she could spare the money to take the bus. It was going to be a long walk home.

A white El Dorado pulled out of the parking lot, accelerating by Natalie. She had a fleeting glimpse of a thin, sensitive face pressed against the window and staring at her before the street lights reduced the two occupants of the car to silhouettes, one large and one small. Red lights from the rear of the car flashed a secret danger signal as the car braked and turned into the sidewalk curb ahead of Natalie. She shifted Ricky in her arms, her heart pounding with fear or pride.

The driver's door was opened and violently slammed shut. As Natalie drew nearer to where the car was parked, she saw the arrogant stranger's long impatient strides eating up the distance that separated them. She could only guess that his daughter had insisted they stop when she recognised Natalie and the sleeping Ricky.

For all the seething fury she had sensed in his movements, the chiselled features that looked at her were remarkably cool and aloof. He stopped directly in her path, forcing her to halt and acknowledge him.

"May we give you a ride to your home?"

The offer was blandly made. Natalie decided that it had been a long time since this man had revealed his true thoughts in his facial expression.

"No, thank you." She spoke concisely and with no hesitation.

She didn't want him to believe for an instant that she might be impressed by his obvious wealth or attention.

"With your son and my daughter as chaperones, I'm hardly likely to do you any harm," he said briskly.

Natalie started to correct him by explaining that Ricky was her nephew, then changed her mind. Let him think what he liked. He probably wouldn't believe her if she told him the truth.

"My daughter is most anxious that you arrive at your home safely." An undercurrent of sarcasm in his voice.

"It was her idea and not yours to stop, too, wasn't it?" Natalie flashed.

"Of course," he agreed, letting her know that the thought would never have occurred to him, just as she had guessed. "And I don't look forward to the prospect of sitting up half the night trying to convince her that you and the boy had come to no harm."

Natalie glanced at the car. The street light illuminated the apprehensive expression of the young face that watched them. It was conceivable that a sensitive young person might be so much concerned.

"We'll accept your offer," Natalie submitted ungraciously.

The slight twist of his mouth informed her that he had expected no other decision. He didn't wait for her as he walked to the car and opened the passenger door. There was a darting smile of gratitude from Missy to him as she scrambled into the back seat, leaving the front seat vacant for Natalie.

The cheap cotton of Natalie's dress slid nearly up to her thigh as she tried to negotiate getting in without disturbing Ricky. Tugging her skirt into a more respectable place, she felt her cheeks stinging with embarrassment, conscious of those cold, watchful eyes that observed everything. Then her door was closed and he was around to the driver's side, sliding behind the wheel.

"Is he asleep?" Missy leaned forward on to the leather armrest in the middle of the front seats.

Natalie pushed back her hostility to answer quietly, "Yes, it's past his bedtime."

The car was in motion, the aristocratic profile concentrating on the traffic and ignoring Natalie completely.

"The parade was nice, wasn't it?" the girl suggested hesitantly as if she wasn't sure of her own opinion.

"Yes," Natalie agreed. "Ricky enjoyed it. It's the first time he's ever seen one."

"Me, too. Except on television," Missy qualified.

"Where do you live?"

Natalie was brought up sharply by the masculine voice, hating herself for forgetting to tell him her address, a situation she quickly corrected.

"Do you know where that is?" she inquired as an afterthought.

"I've lived near San Antonio all my life. There are few places I don't know," he replied evenly.

And yet it was the first time his daughter had been to a Fiesta parade, Natalie added to herself. Her arm brushed the expensive leather upholstery. The failure couldn't have been due to a lack of money, of that she was certain.

"Have you lived here long?" the girl whispered—Natalie had the impression that it was because of her father and not the sleeping child.

"For the last few years," Natalie admitted in an equally quiet voice.

"It's nice. I like San Antonio."

Then Natalie remembered the slight qualification when the man had said that he lived "near" San Antonio. "Ricky said your name was Missy, is that right?"

"Missy Langston, short for Melissa," she explained. Her hand made a slight, hesitant movement in her father's direction. "Th-This is my father, Colter Langston."

The name registered vaguely in Natalie's memory as belonging to someone of importance. She glanced briefly in his direction and found lazy green-blue eyes returning her look. The knowing glitter forced her to look away. He had seen the faint glimmer of recognition cross her face.

"My name is Natalie Crane," she identified herself for no other reason than to fill the suffocating silence.

"Ricky calls you Nonnie, doesn't he?" Missy replied.

A small smile pulled up the corners of her mouth as her fingers touched the head of the boy sleeping against her shoulder.

"When he was smaller, he couldn't say Natalie. That was the closest he could come to it."

"Which of these places is your home?" Colter Langston had made the turn off the main thoroughfare on to the side-street where she and Ricky lived.

"The third house on the right," Natalie answered.

The windows of the large structure were dark except for one small light in the rear. Natalie was glad. Lights would only make the old monstrosity of a house, the upper floors remodelled into apartments, look as shabby and neglected as the darkness hinted. She wished now she had asked to be let out on the corner. She had caught the faint note of derision in his question.

The car stopped next to the curb. Natalie was fumbling for the door handles as the headlights and motor were switched off. Her startled gaze watched Colter Langston get out of the car and walk round to her side. As she realized that this show of courtesy was for his daughter's benefit, her mouth tightened grimly. When her door was opened, she swung her legs around to step out.

"Give me the boy," Colter Langston ordered, his strong hands reaching for Ricky's small waist.

"I can carry him," she asserted firmly, drawing back from the outstretched hands.

"And get your key out of your purse and fumble with the door," he mocked, drawing the boy away from her. "I sincerely doubt that you want me rummaging through your purse for the key.''

Without being encumbered with Ricky, Natalie was quickly out of the car, glaring resentfully at the man so casually holding her sleeping nephew. She walked swiftly and familiarly over the broken concrete walk to the door, long, cat-like strides keeping pace behind her. For once the key didn't stick in the lock, but turned instantly, opening the front door. A step inside, Natalie turned to take Ricky.

''He's fine,'' Colter stated. ''Just point out your apartment.''

''It's upstairs,'' she sighed, wondering if it gave him some sensation of superiority to see how humble her home was. She was simply too tired to care.

As she started towards the stairs, a door into the hallway opened and the iron-grey eyes of her landlady peered out. A brow arched upwards as she spotted the man with Natalie.

''I have told you repeatedly, Miss Crane, that I will not allow you to entertain men in your apartment. This is a respectable house!'' Her landlady's voice rang out harshly.

Through sheer force of will, Natalie held her temper. The first of the month was coming shortly. If she hoped to gain a couple of days' grace to raise the rent money, she couldn't afford to become angry.

"He's only carrying Ricky to my room. He'll be leaving immediately, Mrs. Thomas," Natalie answered, her gaze flickering briefly to Colter Langston.

"Well, see that he does!" the woman snapped and closed the door.

Natalie didn't want to guess what construction Colter Langston had put on the exchange that he had so aloofly observed. If she knew, she would almost certainly tell him just what she thought of his lordly ways.

At the top of the stairs, she unlocked the door to her one-room flat and reached for Ricky. Colter handed him to her without protest.

"Thank you for the ride," she offered grudgingly.

"I'll pass it on to Missy. It was her idea." A subtle reminder that she truly hadn't needed, and he was going back down the steps.

CHAPTER TWO

"You sit here quietly, Ricky, and eat your sandwich," Natalie instructed. "And don't bother anybody."

"I won't," his bright voice promised as he crawled on to the long bench, his chin barely above the wooden counter. "Aren't you going to eat with me, Nonnie?"

"No, honey, I have to work." Honey-brown hair was curling about her face and neck from the heat of the grill. She tried pushing it away from her face, but it was too thick and full to stay there.

Under the influence of her encouraging smile, Ricky picked up the sandwich, cut into sections for his small fingers to handle, and began eating with his usual gusto. The smile faded as Natalie turned away. Her temples throbbed from the heat and excessive noise. The air was stiflingly still with little promise of coolness from the setting sun.

A country-western band was playing a rousing tune in the main square of La Villita. The music was loud to be heard over the steady din of voices and laughter of the milling crowd. "A Night in Old San Antonio", part of the Fiesta week activities, transformed La Villita, a re-creation of the small settlement that once ex-isted there, into four nights of perpetual chaos. Every available inch of space was used for booths to sell ethnic food, drink and gifts na-tive to the various immigrant people who had settled the land.

It was in a stand located in the Frontier sec-tion that Natalie had at last found work. Tem-porary, only for the four nights, but it would be an income, however small. The owner-operator of the stand had raised no objections when Natalie had asked to bring Ricky with her as long as he stayed out of the way. It had saved the considerable expense of a babysitter even if it did mean keeping Ricky up much later than she liked. It was only going to be for four nights and he could always curl up on the bales of hay behind the stand if he became too tired.

Turning another ranch steak on the grill, Natalie wearily wiped the perspiration from her forehead. She had a sinking feeling that all her efforts were in vain. In the last year, everything had seemed to go from bad to worse.

She had grown to love Ricky tremendously and she refused to grumble at the awesome responsibility her love brought. If only she could have an hour's rest from the pressure of her problems, she thought wistfully. If only she didn't feel so unbearably tired and worn out all the time, maybe she could think of a solution. What fun it would be to join in the merriment of the hundreds of people roaming through La Villita, seemingly without a care.

Dully Natalie glanced over her shoulder to be sure that Ricky was still sitting at the counter. At the reassuring sight of the silky brown head, she started to turn back, only to freeze into stillness as her gaze became locked by a pair of aloof green-blue eyes. A wildfire of dislike raced through her veins, amber flames brightening her hazel eyes.

His indifferent study of her was disturbing and Natalie found it impossible to meet it any longer. She let her gaze swing from Colter Langston to his daughter Missy, who was sitting on the bench next to Ricky, smiling shyly and talking to him in a low voice.

Averting her head with a jerky movement, Natalie concentrated her attention on the small steaks on the grill. What bitter irony to see him again! The feeling was mutual, Natalie was sure, that is if the man possessed any feelings. His handsome face was chiselled into cold, ruthless lines, the deep tan of his complexion offsetting the glacial shade of his eyes and the streaks of sun-gold in his hair. Lean and supple, he had the sinewy build of an athlete, or more figuratively, the latent muscular power of a cougar.

Yes, Natalie decided grimly, there was a great deal about him that reminded her of a predatory cat. The nobly proud and withdrawn look in his impassive expression, the air of supreme independence, the strength that was held in check until it was needed, then to be unleashed with lightning swiftness, the dangerous claws that seemed to be sheathed for the time being, the indifference to others' wishes unless it pleased him to indulge them, and, most of all, there was that hint of a primitive animal, undomesticated and disdainful of civilisation. Yet, in spite of it all, Colter Langston possessed a magnetic, almost hypnotic fascination, a kind of frightening lure of danger.

Natalie shook her head firmly to halt the fanciful imaginings of her mind. It was sheer chance that she had seen him again, chance and his daughter's acquaintance with Ricky, and the Fiesta. Her mouth twisted wryly as she realized that for a few moments her money worries had been set aside.

"Nonnie?" Ricky's voice rang clear and sharp, only vaguely apologetic for interrupting her.

After dishing up two more plates, Natalie self-consciously wiped her hands on the gingham checked apron and walked to the counter where Ricky was seated, deliberately ignoring the man standing behind him.

"Hello, Missy," she greeted the girl quietly, and received a hesitant nod in return.

"I ate all my dinner." Ricky pushed the clean plate forward for her inspection. Before Natalie could comment, he rushed on, "Missy said she would take me around and show me everything."

"I'll keep hold of his hand all the time so he won't get lost," Missy inserted anxiously.

"I'm sure you would be very careful, Missy, but—" Natalie began her denial. She glanced unwillingly at the emotionless, masculine face above the two children seated at the counter. "I think Ricky should stay here with me. It's very crowded tonight."

"Oh, Daddy!" Missy turned her anxious pleading face to Colter Langston, who viewed it without a flicker of interest. "Please make Mrs. Crane understand that we would take care of him."

Natalie squirmed inwardly, knowing what a difficult position Missy was placing both of them in. She didn't have to hear him speak to know that the last thing Colter Langston wanted to do was squire her nephew around. His aloof gaze swung to her and Natalie steeled herself to meet it.

"The boy will be quite safe with us. We'll bring him directly back here once we've made the tour, Mrs. Crane," he stated with a trace of mocking inflection on the word "Mrs."

"It's *Miss* Crane. Ricky is my nephew." The brief arching of his brow made Natalie regret that she had corrected him. "Now, if you'll excuse me, I have to get back to work."

"We'll bring Ricky back in an hour," Colter responded smoothly.

"I didn't say he could go!" Natalie turned back in astonishment.

"The child has little else to do while you're working. What's the harm?" he challenged.

Resentment flared unchecked in her gaze, but it made little impression on him. She couldn't stand there and argue the point, especially in front of the two children watching the exchange so closely. Indecision hovered in her mind until she met the pair of pleading brown eyes, so loving and full of mischief. It would serve Colter Langston right to take Ricky.

"All right," she sighed agreement. "I'll expect Ricky back in an hour."

Afterwards she wondered if she had been insane to agree. Colter Langston and his daughter were virtual strangers, regardless of how respectable they appeared on the surface. ''Respectable''—it was hardly an adjective that could be applied to him, not with any degree of certainty.

Yet there was the unshakeable impression that Colter Langston had been selfishly indulging the whim of his daughter, using Ricky to entertain her so he wouldn't have to. The more Natalie thought about that the more positive she became that it had been his only motive.

As the hour neared its end, Natalie kept searching the crowd, now grown to such proportions that they were elbow to elbow as they jostled their way to the various ethnic booths. The sky had darkened to a purpling black and La Villita was illuminated by strings of brightly coloured lights strung across squares and alleys and atop the booths. The time for her fifteen-minute break was approaching, precious minutes that she wanted to devote to Ricky.

Then, through the mob of people young and old, Natalie saw him perched again on Colter's arm as the three wound their way to the stand. Colter's hand firmly kept Missy directly in front of him. Ricky's brown eyes were round and wondering at all the things he had seen. She knew he would talk non-stop for an hour to share his tour with her. Even Missy's face was unusually animated and happy.

Ricky almost leaped into her outstretched arms. "Did you have a good time?" Natalie smiled.

"Terrific!" he breathed, and would have launched into a full account then and there, but Missy broke in.

"We brought him back safely," she offered earnestly.

"Yes, you did." Her gaze flickered automatically from the girl to her father, her smile turning a little more reserved under his lazy, yet piercing look. "Thank you."

Natalie stood Ricky up on an empty corner of the counter bench, tucking his shirt tail back into his trousers. "You should have seen the pretty eggs," he told her excitedly.

"'Cascarones'," Missy added, more fully identifying the confetti-filled eggshells for Natalie's benefit.

"You break them over people's heads!" His dark, bright eyes rounded still more as Ricky passed on that startling discovery to Natalie. She couldn't help laughing at his amazed expression, the laughter erasing the lines of concern.

Missy reached into the small straw purse she was carrying and took out a red and a blue "cascarone". "You can take these home with you, if you like, Ricky," she offered.

Natalie's hand was resting lightly on Ricky's back. She felt him stiffen slightly, drawing himself more erect. She glanced curiously at his solemn expression as he stared at the brightly coloured eggshells in Missy's hand.

"Nonnie and me, we don't accept charity."

A warm flush of embarrassment crept up her cheeks at the almost physical touch of the mocking gaze that was directed at her. It was so obvious that Ricky was repeating an admonition he had heard her say many times. She felt even worse when she saw the hurt look steal over Missy's face, the sparkle leaving her blue eyes.

"It's not charity." Colter's low voice, calm and unruffled, drew Ricky's gaze. "It's a Fiesta gift, just like at Christmas time."

Barely moving his head, he turned to Natalie for confirmation of Colter's words. When it had been a simple, inexpensive gift from Missy, Natalie had not minded Ricky accepting the "cascarones". Now that her father had involved himself, she wanted to refuse. Her denial would not affect Colter Langston who was only backing up his daughter as she would have done in his place, but it would be one more simple treat that she couldn't give Ricky. She wished the innocent children did not have to suffer from the actions of an adult.

"That's right, Ricky," Natalie agreed grudgingly. "Why don't you go get your truck and show it to Missy?"

Carefully cradling the "cascarones" in his hand, the little boy took off like a shot for the toy truck placed for safe keeping behind the counter. Apart from that one comment, Colter Langston did not take part again in the three-way conversation of Natalie, Missy and Ricky, but Natalie never lost her awareness of him, her nerve ends tingling whenever she felt his dispassionate gaze directed at her.

Her break was over and she was back working at the grill when Missy said goodbye to Ricky. Natalie doubted that Colter Langston had joined in the farewell. She was certain any courtesy had been extended by Missy.

As she had suspected, Ricky curled up very willingly on the bale of straw to the back of the stand—to watch the people, he said. Shortly after ten o'clock, she saw his head drooping in sleep. A few minutes later, he had shifted into a horizontal position; sleeping away completely unmindful of the din that hadn't let up since the gates of La Villita had opened up at five-thirty that afternoon.

Officially, the celebration of "A Night in Old San Antonio" ended at ten-thirty each night, but it was closer to eleven-thirty before the grill was cleaned and Natalie was able to leave. The last three days she had spent in an exhaustive search for a new job. That combined with almost six straight hours on her feet over the sapping heat of the grill made her feel too weary to take another step. Time enough to collapse when she reached home, Natalie told herself firmly, and picked up Ricky and his truck and her purse to trudge to the gates of the Alamo Street entrance.

Just as she stepped through them, a tall figure pushed itself away from the stone walls of La Villita. Her tired brain identified Colter Langston a second before he lifted the sleeping child from her unprotesting arms.

"My car is across the street."

"You don't have to—" Natalie began feebly.

His head was drawn back slightly, heightening the effect that he was looking down at her. "Would you like a ride home or not? A simple 'yes' or 'no' will do." The pitch of his low voice didn't change, yet there was an underlying harshness to it.

The prospect of the long walk to her apartment looked more daunting than a short ride with Colter Langston. Besides, in her weak-ened state, she found his strength and vitality intimidated her. Natalie held his cold, expressionless gaze for an instant.

"Missy's idea, I suppose," she sighed, unable to acquiesce completely, and he didn't deny her observation. Wearily she pushed the hair away from her face. "Yes, we will accept your offer."

"My car is across the street," Colter repeated.

Natalie had no trouble finding the white El Dorado in the half-empty parking lot. Once she was in the passenger seat, he handed the sleeping Ricky to her and walked around to the driver's side. As Natalie tried to shift Ricky into a more comfortable position on her lap, his eyes blinked open.

Craning his head around, he looked into the back seat, then at Colter. "Where's Missy?"

"She's in bed, asleep." Colter answered the question as if it had been asked by an adult.

"I'm tired, too," Ricky agreed, and settled his head against Natalie's shoulder, dropping off almost instantly to sleep.

Natalie leaned her own head against the rich leather cushions, half-closing her eyes as the powerful car accelerated into the street. The darkness and quietness outside closed around her like a warm cocoon.

"I never realised silence could be so beautiful," she murmured aloud, "or so peaceful."

The unceasing din of the crowds took on the aspects of a nightmare that was only barely remembered. Out of the corner of her eye, she studied his profile. The softly firm cushion of seat relaxed her tired muscles, lessening their ache, and Natalie felt a twinge of conscience that she hadn't expressed her gratitude for the ride more graciously.

"I do appreciate your taking Ricky and me home, Mr. Langston. I hope your wife doesn't object."

The last remark, incuriously offered, twisted the hard line of his mouth into a mirthless smile as he ran an eye over her face. "I doubt it. She's dead."

The callous announcement astounded Natalie. "I—I'm sorry," she said, for want of any other response.

"Are you?" His gaze never left the street. "Why? Because she's dead or because I can't pretend to feel any grief over something that happened more than ten years ago?" Colter asked with asperity.

There was no answer Natalie could give to the frank question, so she subsided into an uneasy silence, a silence the taciturn man appeared to endorse. She didn't need to have a picture drawn to realise that Colter Langston did not indulge in idle conversation. He was brutally frank and straight to the point. Her unconscious probe into his personal life had been reversed as dexterously as an expert swordsman parries the thrust of an amateur.

When they arrived at the house where she lived, again Colter took Ricky from her while she retrieved her key from the scant contents of her purse. The landlady's hallway door opened a crack for her stern face to peer out, but mercifully she said nothing, letting her presence serve as a reminder of her admonition the night before.

As Natalie hurried up the stairs to her apartment, her tired legs stumbled over a step near the top. Instantly a firm hand was under her elbow, righting her. The hard strength and warm support that it represented was so overwhelming that Natalie wished she could lean against it if only for a moment. She pushed away the impulse and the hand was withdrawn almost immediately.

The door of her apartment opened wider than she intended, allowing an unobstructed view of the sparsely furnished but clean room. In the short time it took to transfer the sleeping child from his arms to hers, Natalie had the feeling that the entire room had been memorised by

Colter's discerning gaze. Her thanks were self-consciously offered and summarily shrugged aside as he turned back down the stairs before she had closed the door.

Each succeeding night of "A Night in Old San Antonio" was a repeat of the first. Colter and Missy arrived at about the same time and Missy spent most of the evening entertaining Ricky while Colter looked on. At closing, he was waiting outside the gates alone to give Natalie a lift home.

Her one offer to pay had been rejected with a derisive glance. After the third night, Natalie had ceased conjecturing that his motive might be more than a way to ease his sensitive daughter's imagination. Working nights, searching without success for a permanent job during the day, and caring for Ricky did not leave many moments for idle thought.

It was approaching midnight when Colter brought her home on Friday, the last night of the festivities at La Villita and the last night of her job. There was a fleeting thought as she took Ricky from his arms that there was little likelihood that she and Ricky would see Colter or Missy again. Before Natalie could utter any final goodbye, he was reaching around her for the doorknob and she realised that he couldn't care less that he wouldn't see her again. That was

fine. Neither did she. She had only been thinking that Ricky might miss his daughter. She
murmured a sharp "Good night" and stepped
into the apartment, adding the weight of her
hand to the back of the door he was already
pulling shut.

Weak and exhausted, wanting nothing more
than to crawl between the covers of the daybed
she shared with Ricky, Natalie instead walked to
the tiny kitchen alcove and put a kettle of water
on the stove to boil. As it heated, she spooned
instant coffee into a cup, gathered pencil and
paper and the pay envelope from her purse and
set them all on the small table. She knew she
wouldn't be able to sleep until she knew the true
state of their finances.

Sipping the deliberately strong coffee later,
Natalie reworked the figures. It didn't seem to
matter how many things she eliminated as non-
essential, there was simply not enough money to
carry them through the next week. In the three
years Ricky had been with her, the future had
never looked as bleak and hopeless as it did at
that moment. Burying her face in her hands, she
began to cry softly, tired sobs and acid tears that
couldn't ease the pain of despair.

The click of the doorknob turning brought
her head up sharply in frightened disbelief. The
lean masculine form of Colter Langston was

framed in the doorway. His keen eyes missed nothing, not the ravages of tears on her face, the small stack of money meticulously counted out, the scribbled figures on the paper, nor the air of defeat in her sagging shoulders.

"What are you doing here?" she breathed.

"You forgot to take the key out of the lock."

There was the jangle of metal as he tossed her key on to the table. When her stunned gaze turned to it, he took the few steps necessary to reach the table and placed a paper package in the middle.

"W-what's that?"

"A sandwich."

"For me?" Natalie stared at the impassive, unyielding face towering above her.

"I had dinner this evening. Did you?" A brow arched inquiringly. "Or did Ricky receive the meal you were entitled to for working at the stand?" Her sharply averted head was the only answer he needed. "I thought as much."

The derisive tone brought an immediate surge of pride. "I'm not hungry," Natalie asserted, trying to ignore the tantalizing aroma that set her stomach gnawing at her backbone.

There was a short exhalation of his breath that bespoke Colter's contempt of her refusal. "Please spare me your little speech about charity. From the boy it was cute. From you, it would be ridiculous!''

Tanned fingers tore open the paper to reveal the two sliced halves of French bread mounded in the middle with barbecued beef. He slid it in front of her, disregarding the neat stacks of money he toppled.

"Eat it," commanded Colter.

The glittering harshness of his gaze told her that he would shove it down her throat if she refused again. Torn between the desire to throw it in his face before he had a chance and to appease the hunger sapping her strength, Natalie stared into the bronze mask.

"What do I owe for your generosity?" she demanded.

An uncomfortable heat warmed her blood as his gaze travelled suggestively over her, insolently noting the feminine curves that her recent loss of weight had only accented. The corners of his hard mouth quirked with dry cynicism at the corners when his gaze returned to her face. Her cheeks still glistened from the tears she had shed, but gold sparks were flashing defiantly from her eyes.

"At least you've learned nothing is for free," he commented. "But all I want for the present is a few minutes to discuss something with you once you've eaten."

"That's all?" Natalie challenged, wary of that vague qualification he had made.

"For the present," Colter repeated, smiling coldly at the indignant flush that was appearing under his pinning gaze. "The eventual outcome of our discussion will be strictly your decision. Does that satisfy you?"

Natalie flinched under his cutting mockery. "Not really." Her eyes unwillingly were drawn to the tempting sandwich.

"Eat. I have no intention of raping you."

His bluntness stole some of her appetite but not a sufficient amount to lessen the hunger pangs. Strangely Natalie believed that he wouldn't attempt to molest her despite the vague feeling that she would be wiser not to hear what he wanted to discuss. At her first bite into the sandwich, Colter moved away from the table.

"What are you doing?" Natalie swallowed the bite quickly, turning in her chair as he walked behind her towards the kitchen alcove.

"Getting myself a cup of coffee."

"I'll do that," she said, quickly setting her sandwich down to push herself away from the table.

But his deceptively effortless strides had already taken him into the small cooking area. "Why, Mother Hubbard? Because your cupboards are bare,'' he answered drily. ''I'd already guessed that.''

As proof he opened the top door beside the sink to reveal the nearly empty shelves. Her pale complexion flamed as she watched him take a cup and spoon in the instant coffee. The kettle heated up again speedily and he poured the scalding water into the cup. As the sun-bleached head turned towards her, Natalie subsided quickly in her chair.

When he wandered back to the table, there was only a faint hint of pink in her cheeks. She studiously avoided looking directly at him as he reclined his lean frame in the straight chair opposite her, relaxing with negligent ease. Eating under his perceptively watchful eye did not aid her digestive abilities.

Natalie started visibly when he leaned forward suddenly, his hand reaching to the side of her. Then she saw the object that had captured his attention, a framed photograph of her brother, his wife and Ricky that sat on the shelf beside the table.

''My brother Ned and his wife Susan taken on Ricky's second birthday,'' Natalie explained defensively when his glance was turned sharply on her.

''Then he is your nephew.''

"Yes, he is." Her chin tilted in proud defiance. "They were killed in a car crash shortly after the picture was taken."

"And Ricky had no other family?"

"Our parents are dead and Susan's mother was an invalid," she responded, wondering why she was answering his probing questions at all.

"You must have been quite young yourself." Colter continued his study of the photograph.

"Eighteen, if it's any of your business," and she was rewarded for her sharpness with an immediate narrowing of his gaze.

But otherwise, his expression remained completely unruffled. "That makes you twenty-one or twenty-two?"

"Twenty-one."

This was not idle table conversation, but serving some purpose that Natalie couldn't begin to perceive. She could only guess that it concerned something that he wanted to discuss with her.

"No boy-friends?"

"No," she answered shortly.

She was unable or unwilling to explain that Ricky's advent into her life had brought a halt to nearly all her social activities, with male or female. A kind of loneliness, however reluctantly acknowledged, had become her constant companion.

"Few young men want the responsibility of another man's child," Colter observed drily, "or the restrictions it places on a girl's social life."

He had put his finger exactly on the problem, but his accurate perception didn't ease her wariness. Natalie refused to acknowledge the truth of his statement and remained silent.

"You're sacrificing quite a lot for the sake of the boy." He had replaced the photograph and was leaning back in the chair, tilting it on its back legs.

" 'The boy' has a name. It's Ricky," Natalie replied tautly, hating the way Colter Langston kept referring to him as if Ricky was an inanimate object. "And I don't regard it as a sacrifice. It isn't Ricky's fault that his parents were killed."

"Nor yours, although you seem determined to make up for it."

"What would you suggest I do?" Natalie demanded angrily. "Turn him over to the courts to be shuffled from one foster home to another without knowing the security of any family?"

"I don't imagine there was anything else you could do under the circumstances." Colter set the chair back on all four legs.

Despite his statement of agreement, Natalie

sensed he didn't agree with her. She thrust the remains of the sandwich impatiently aside, losing her taste for any more of it.

CHAPTER THREE

"WOULD YOU mind telling me exactly what it is that you came to discuss?" Natalie challenged, tired of playing the game of being mouse to his cat.

Impassive and unrelenting, the bronze mask stared back at her. The only life to his expression was in the frosty glitter of his eyes. Even that was unreadable.

"This evening," his hand moved the coffee cup away from the edge of the table, "Missy told me that she wished her mother had not died giving birth to her. Hardly an unusual comment for a child to make, I'll admit, but her reason for the statement was that she would have liked to have had a little brother or sister. She's become very fond of your nephew."

"I'm sorry if that has inconvenienced you," Natalie retaliated.

Sympathy rose for Missy, who had probably been taught by her father not to expect too much affection from adults, especially parents.

His gaze narrowed. "We live on a ranch. My aunt, who lives with us, takes care of Missy," continued Colter. "She's quite elderly. It's becoming increasingly difficult for her to do all the cooking and cleaning, etcetera, that's required. She has expressed a wish to retire, you might say."

"I see," Natalie murmured. The picture had begun to form in her mind. He was seeking a replacement for his aunt, someone to take care of his house and his daughter. "And that's what you want to talk to me about."

"Exactly." There was a faintly amused twist of his mouth. "If you'll pardon the understatement, life hasn't been easy for you and the boy. And from the frantic scribbles on that paper, the future doesn't look very bright either."

"If you mean, do I need a job? the answer is yes."

"It isn't a job I'm offering you."

It was difficult for Natalie to hold that level, ever-watchful gaze. She took a deep breath, feeling inexplicably tired of trying to match wits with someone who obviously was always one step ahead of her.

"Then what is all this leading to?" Natalie asked, wearily exhaling the breath she had just taken.

"I want you to marry me." There was not the slightest change in his bland, unemotional tone, nor did his eyes waver from her face.

She blinked and frowned. "Is that some kind of a joke?"

"I'm completely serious." Now that the announcement had been made and her reaction studied, Colter Langston reached into his pocket for a cigarette and a lighter.

"But I don't love you, and you certainly don't love me," Natalie returned in blank confusion.

"Hardly." The idea that she might have thought he did struck a chord of perverted amusement, revealed in silent laughter.

Natalie couldn't see the funny side. "I thought you said you needed a housekeeper and someone to look after Missy," she reminded him with a trace of anger.

"I do." Calmly he blew a cloud of grey smoke above the table. "That's why I want to marry you."

Her mouth felt dry and cottony. With a flash of irritation, she rose from the table, taking her cup and walking into the small alcove for more much-needed coffee.

"I'm afraid I don't see your reasoning," she said shortly. "You don't have to acquire a wife to obtain a housekeeper."

"Don't I?" His low, drawling voice, cynically tinged with mockery, carried across the room. "I want to be assured that whoever I get will be more or less permanent. Housekeepers tend to give notice. It's much easier to sever the strings of employment than it is the bonds of matrimony."

"Marriage—that's rather a drastic measure just to keep a housekeeper, isn't it?" Natalie suggested drily as she poured water into the crystals of instant coffee.

"Not drastic, practical," corrected Colter.

"I think the whole idea is ridiculous!" With an impatient sigh, she began stirring the brown liquid.

When Colter had mentioned that he needed a housekeeper, she had wanted the job, her heart leaping at the thought of Ricky living in the country and herself being there whenever he needed her. But this marriage was something else again.

"Why is it ridiculous? You need a job and I need a housekeeper. I've already seen that you work hard." His gaze swept over the small apartment. "You're tidy and clean. You are obviously very fond of children and they return it—or at least your nephew does, and Missy is less silent with you than with most adults. I presume you can cook?"

"Yes, I can cook, but—" Leaning a hip against the counter, Natalie waved a hand in the air helplessly, "but there must be half a dozen girls willing to marry you. Girls much more suitable than I am."

"Not more suitable." He rolled lazily to his feet, picking up his own empty coffee cup and walking to the alcove where Natalie stood. "Better dressed, maybe, educated in better schools, from a different social sphere, and all of them could probably convince themselves that they're in love with me, or the Langston name and money. I don't want or need their love."

There was such a decided sneer given to the last word that Natalie couldn't help adding coldly, "Or anyone's?"

"Does that shock you?" His eyes glittered over her face. "Nearly the entire world lives under that cloud of deceit."

She had wondered before if he had any feelings. Now she knew he hadn't, not any of any depth at least. "You don't want a wife. You want a slave," she accused.

"It's illegal," Colter returned without a lash flickering.

Natalie breathed in sharply with disgust. "I can't believe you seriously expect me to agree to your proposal."

"Why? It's not without compensations to you. You and the boy will not lack for material needs—food, clothing, shelter, instead of a hand-to-mouth existence. I can provide the financial means for him to have a higher education if he wants it. In other words, all your worries will be gone. You'll have nothing to concern yourself about except taking care of my home and Missy. Other than the times the boy is in school, he'll be with you constantly."

It was a very tempting picture he painted and he knew its lure. What hope did she have to do as much for Ricky? What did the future hold for her but more nerve-racking days wondering how she was going to pay for some bill or put food on their table and a roof over their heads?

"What's the matter?" Colter asked drily. "Are you still nourishing some childhood dream that Prince Charming will appear and carry you off into the sunset?" Natalie flashed him a resentful look. "When was the last time you had a date?"

Despite the mutinous line of her mouth that longed to deny the arrogant certainty of his gaze, she averted her head.

"Over two years ago," she admitted grudgingly. "Doesn't it bother you that your friends would think it strange for you to marry someone like me?'' she added, attempting to shift the subject from her social life, or lack of one.

''Why should they? You're an attractive girl. Tired and overworked, in need of rest and more meat on your bones and more attractive clothes to cover you.'' His hand closed over her chin, twisting her face around to see it better. ''In fact, you could be quite beautiful. The gold dust in your almond eyes and the sensual fullness of your lips would arouse any man's desire. Our marriage would probably be regarded as very romantic.''

His detached appraisal was disturbing, but not nearly so much as her rocketing pulse at his touch. In all the impressions Natalie had formed, she had forgotten or ignored his overpowering masculinity, the supreme dominating maleness. It was his virile attraction that held the element of danger she had sensed. And Natalie was susceptible—she could feel it in the sudden heightening of her senses. She was a female who had been too long without the attentions of a male.

Trying to fight back that discovery, she wrenched her head from his hold. ''Next you'll be examining my teeth like a horse!'' she flared.

Colter leaned against the edge of the counter, disregarding her sarcasm. ''The marriage would be convenient for both of us. It wouldn't raise near as many eyebrows as hiring you strictly as a housekeeper would.''

''It's insane,'' Natalie denied, staring at her cooling cup of coffee.

''It's logical. What's your answer?''

''I need time to think.'' Although she wasn't sure what there was to think about, except that she was reluctant to say ''no''.

''I don't have time. Missy and I are leaving for the ranch on Sunday morning. That only leaves tomorrow. There are certain arrangements that can't be postponed till the last minute,'' Colter informed her, his arms folded in front of him.

''You can't expect me to give you an answer now,'' Natalie responded, nervously running her fingers through her brown hair.

''I can and I do.'' There was an underlying thread of impatience in his voice. ''What are your alternatives? You've had time enough tonight before I came back to assess what the future holds for you in the present circumstances.'' He straightened from the counter, towering above her. ''I'm leaving, Natalie Crane, and I want your answer before I walk through the door.''

Her gaze flew to his face in disbelief, the cold, impassive face, the handsome lines etched with unrelenting firmness. He held her gaze for an instant, letting her see that he meant exactly what he said. Then his lithe, supple strides were carrying him towards the door without a backward glance.

At the click of the doorknob, Natalie's paralysis ended. "Yes."

Colter turned, his arrogant expression unchanged, not a trace of satisfaction or any other emotion.

"I'll pick you and the boy up at eight tomorrow morning." His gaze made an all-encompassing sweep of the room. "You won't be coming back here, so pack only what you need or want to keep. I wouldn't be concerned about clothes. You'll both be getting new wardrobes."

Without giving Natalie a chance to reply or bidding her goodnight, he was out of the door, his cat-soft footsteps sounding faintly on the stairs. She leaned weakly against the counter, her eyes turning towards the sleeping child.

"Have I done the right thing?" she murmured aloud, then turned her eyes towards the ceiling. "Oh, God, have I done the right thing?" The only response to her whispered prayer was the sound of a powerful engine springing to life in the street below.

Natalie had expected to spend a restless night, plagued by doubts about her and Ricky's future, but she slept the sleep of the innocent. For the first time in recent memory, she awoke feeling refreshed and rested without that heavy weight of responsibility pushing her down. A marriage of convenience didn't sound quite as bad as it had last night.

Omitting their clothing and sparse household goods, there was little to pack. But the process wasn't speeded up by Ricky's unbounded excitement, generated not by Natalie's announcement that she was going to marry Missy's father, but by all the changes that were brought by it.

"Can I really have a pair of cowboy boots?" he asked for the hundredth time, Natalie was sure.

"Yes." She smiled patiently, unable and unwilling to dampen his enthusiasm. "As long as you're a good boy. Are you sure you have all your toys in the sack?"

"Yes," Ricky sighed contentedly.

Apprehensions churned her stomach when Colter knocked on the door promptly at eight o'clock. Before the doubts could take hold, he had them and their few belongings stowed in the car, and the landlady cuttingly dealt with.

The entire day was a whirl of efficient organization, never allowing Natalie more than a passing opportunity to think about what she was doing. An entire wardrobe had been chosen by Colter, from the most intimate lingerie to accessories for an evening dress. While Natalie had her hair shampooed, styled and set, the same impersonal attention was given to Ricky's clothing needs, fortunately including a pair of cowboy boots.

She had barely caught her breath at lunch before Colter was whisking the four of them on to a chartered jet bound for Laredo and ultimately, by rented car, to Nuevo Laredo across the border in Mexico, where she and Colter were married. In the car and on the flight to and from Laredo, Missy and Ricky had kept up a steady stream of chatter in which Ricky always included Natalie but Colter was left out.

That evening the events of the day took on an unreal quality as if none of it had happened except in a dream. Breathing deeply of the warm night air, Natalie glanced at her dusty-coloured apricot pants suit, the elegant lines complementing her slender and curvaceous figure.

It had all happened. There was a heavy gold band on her finger to prove that she was Mrs. Colter Langston. And there was Ricky standing in front of her beside Missy, staring down again at the pointed toes of his shiny new cowboy boots.

Her gold-flecked eyes were directed curiously at Colter a foot or more to her right. As he had all day, he appeared aloof, detached from the group while in command of them. The casual suit that he wore with such negligent ease was cream-coloured, accenting the streaks of gold in his hair and pointing out the pale colour of his eyes against the dark tan of his skin. As if sensing her inspection, his eyes, hesitating closer to green than blue tonight, swung their gaze to Natalie from the precision drill teams entertaining the crowd.

"It's too late for second thoughts," he told her quietly.

Under his compelling gaze, Natalie couldn't look away. "It's too soon to say whether I regret it," she answered truthfully. She tilted her head to one side, her face softly illuminated by an overhead street light, her hair in its new flattering style glistening with a golden glow, the total effect feminine and unconsciously alluring. "Do you?"

The mask of his expression didn't vary as his gaze raked her from head to toe. "I never regret anything," Colter replied.

"How wonderful it must be to be that confident," she mused.

"The only time you regret something is when your emotions are involved."

"And you don't have any emotions?" Natalie mocked the implacable mask.

"No, that curse wasn't put on me when I was born."

Automatically her gaze shifted to Missy, protectively holding Ricky's hand. "You don't feel anything?"

He guessed she was referring to his daughter. "Responsibility." Amusement flickered faintly around the corners of his mouth. "That shocks you, too."

"That's hard to comprehend." A frown of concentration drew her finely arched brows together. "Have you never cared deeply for anyone—your parents, your wife?"

Muscular shoulders moved in a careless shrug as he turned away, letting a sideways glance slide back to her face. "I don't particularly care for myself. It's just as well you should discover that about me now, Natalie." It still sounded strange to hear him say her name. It sounded as if he wasn't actually talking to her, a name that belonged to someone else. "That way you won't expect very much from our marriage."

If her subconscious had formulated any thought that something might grow between them, it died with his statement. There was a slight easing of her conscience at the same time. It wasn't a loveless marriage but a true marriage of convenience where each of them received what they wanted and expected no more.

"Look, Nonnie!" Ricky instructed excitedly. "The parade is going to start."

Obediently Natalie directed her gaze to the street and the university marching band that had assembled. Beyond them and the crowd lining the opposite side of the street was the spotlighted façade of the Alamo, the cradle and shrine of Texas liberty, the focal point of all the Fiesta activities celebrating Texas's independence from Mexico. The strategic Long Barrack stood watch to the side.

A drum roll from the band silenced the crowd as it anticipated the first notes of the song. In the hush of the Alamo, the strains of "The Eyes of Texas Are Upon You" filled the air, inspiring and proud. As Natalie stood a little bit straighter, she was conscious of a pair of Texas eyes on her. She glanced at Colter, applause and cheers rippling through the crowd when the song ended. His vague air of boredom dampened her enthusiasm for the Fiesta Flambeau, the night parade marking the official end of the Fiesta.

This time Ricky stayed awake through the entire parade, although by the time they arrived at the hotel, his eyelids were beginning to droop. Hotel rooms during Fiesta had been booked months in advance, but Colter had used his money or influence to obtain a room with twin beds on the floor below his.

This was not how Natalie had envisioned her wedding night—with her husband one floor above her, but then she had never expected to be left with Ricky to care for when she had indulged in her romantic imaginings. Nor had she expected to marry a man she didn't love. She didn't mind, she told herself as she slipped the expensively flimsy nightgown over her head and climbed into bed. Ricky was happy and that was all she had a right to ask for.

It was midmorning before she awoke. Natalie doubted if she would have then if Ricky hadn't hopped on to the bed, hungry and eager to be off to the ranch that Missy had told him about. Colter and Missy were both in the lobby when she and Ricky hurried down.

"I'm sorry. I overslept," Natalie apologised.

"You needed the rest." Colter dismissed her apology in that offhand, indifferent way she was beginning to expect. "If your luggage is packed, I'll send the bellboy to the room. We'll leave as soon as you and Ricky have breakfasted."

Natalie assured him that all was in readiness. There was a fluttering of nerves as she watched him walk away, realising that within a couple of hours she would be on his ranch, in charge of his home. And his daughter, she added.

Missy was already taking Ricky by the hand to lead him into the hotel restaurant. The marriage hadn't bothered her in the slightest. The only one Missy seemed interested in was Ricky. Natalie guessed it was because the young girl could lavish on the small boy all the love and attention that her father had rejected.

Colter joined them at the breakfast table for coffee. Natalie discovered, to her surprise, that she wasn't at all nervous with him. She had expected to be. They were married and they were strangers. For the next few years at least, they were going to share the same house and food, even if not the same bed. It was a marvel that she was taking the situation so calmly. Perhaps the shock had not worn off.

With all four of them sitting at the breakfast table, they looked like a complete family unit. Not boisterously happy, as families are romantically depicted, because Missy had that shy withdrawn look she always wore in public places, and Colter, taciturn and implacable, held himself slightly aloof. Yet the naturalness of their image wouldn't leave Natalie.

As soon as the meal was finished, they left for the ranch. Some of Ricky's excitement over their soon-to-be-seen new home rubbed off on to Natalie. She longed to question Colter about it, but she decided against it. He might consider her questions more mercenary than curious.

Once the city of San Antonio was left behind the scenery claimed her attention. It had been so long since she had been in the country that the spacious expanse of blue sky stretching above rolling, timbered hills took her breath away. More spectacular were the limitless fields of spring wildflowers, sometimes dotting, sometimes filling entire valley meadows. Set off by the green of the grass, they were vividly bright, ranging from whites, oranges, yellows, pinks to the ever favourite sky-blue of the bluebonnet.

"How much farther?" Ricky piped up from the back seat, dodging the extra cases that wouldn't fit in the already full trunk.

"A few more miles," Colter replied.

"How far is the ranch from San Antonio?" It hadn't seemed as though they had travelled very far from San Antonio and Natalie couldn't prevent herself from asking the question.

"Somewhere around sixty miles." He was slowing the car and turning on to one of the lesser ranch roads that intersected the main highway.

"You could have easily driven back and forth to the Fiesta," she responded without thinking.

"I believe Missy thought she would miss something." Colter glanced in the rear view mirror at his daughter who was listening patiently to Ricky. "The only thing she might have missed was meeting the boy."

The dryness of his tone forced Natalie to ask: "Are you sorry?"

"No." A brow arched briefly in her direction. "Are you?"

"No," she answered quietly, feeling strangely tranquil.

Within a few minutes, the car slowed again and turned on to a gravelled road, gliding dusty white beneath tall crossbars that heralded the entrance to the Langston Ranch. The road sloped gradually upwards leading towards a stand of tall trees. Through their branches, Natalie caught a glimpse of dark red and, as they drew closer, a smattering of ivory white. Guessing at Colter's wealth had not prepared her for the sight of the sprawling ranch house that lay beneath the towering trees.

Thoroughly modern, its style was traditionally Spanish with red-tiled roof and smooth stucco walls, scrolling wrought iron at the windows. Flowering brushes and shrubs abounded in exotic profusion, their vibrant flowers accented by the enormous white blossoms of a magnolia tree. The lane curved towards the house, then continued on through the stand of trees descending the slight slope they had climbed.

"We're home," Missy announced unnecessarily.

As Colter braked the car to a halt in front of the stone walkway leading to the house, a man came walking through the trees towards them— tall, broad-chested, wings of white mingled with otherwise dark hair beneath a western hat brim, older than Colter, perhaps in his late thirties.

"I see you're back, Colter," the man said as Colter stepped from the car and walked to greet him. "I was just coming up to the house to check."

Missy and Ricky were faster getting out of the car than Natalie, who dawdled to get a longer look at the sprawling, elegant ranch house that was her new home. She missed hearing Colter's reply as she closed the car door.

"Did you enjoy the Fiesta, moppet?" The man tugged Missy's long braid as she walked by him to her father.

"Yes," she answered politely, giving him a shy smile.

Ricky too had been taking in the sights and for once lagged behind Missy. His silky brown head was trying to turn simultaneously in all directions and still see where he was going, without success.

"Hello there," the man greeted him when Ricky almost ran into him. "And who are you?"

"My name is Ricky," he announced unabashedly, taking his measure of the stranger. "I think I'm going to live here."

The man glanced curiously at Colter, then caught Natalie's approach out of the corner of his eye. The boy was forgotten as he studied her, and Natalie felt herself blossoming warmly under his admiring gaze. His brown eyes were telling her, respectfully, that he found her very attractive, but they didn't leave her with the feeling that she had been undressed. Instinctively Natalie knew she was going to like this man, whoever he was.

"Travis, I'd like you to meet my wife Natalie. Her nephew has already introduced himself, I believe," Colter stated. "Natalie, my foreman, Travis McCrea."

If a thunderbolt had struck him, the attractive stranger couldn't have been more shocked. As self-conscious pink began to appear in Natalie's cheeks, he tried to hide his amazement.

"Forgive me," he asked Natalie. "I didn't realise Colter had any plans to marry again."

"That's quite all right," Natalie replied after Colter had failed to comment on his foreman's observation.

"Travis usually eats with us if he's around the house at mealtimes," Colter informed her. "You can file that away for future reference."

"If you have any objections to that arrangement," Travis McCrea interjected, "I can make other plans."

"None at all," Natalie assured him with a genuine smile. "I hope you'll continue the practice, Mr. McCrea."

"Travis," he corrected, her smile immediately bringing an answering one on his tanned face. "We aren't formal at the ranch."

"Then call me Natalie."

"Thank you, I will." There was a curious glint in his dark eyes when he glanced briefly at Colter, but it was gone when he directed his warm brown gaze at Natalie. "You'll be anxious to see your new home. I won't keep you, Colter." He touched his hat with his finger and returned the way he had come.

"You liked him, didn't you?" Colter commented smoothly as they turned to follow the children to the house.

"Is there any reason why I shouldn't?" Natalie countered, wondering why she was on the defensive simply because she had immediately liked Travis McCrea.

"No."

"Then why did you ask?"

"A lot of women find him attractive," was the only reply she received.

"I would imagine so," Natalie agreed, striving for a noncommittal tone.

His inscrutable gaze swung at her, frostily cool and aloof. "Why do you feel guilty because you were attracted to him?"

"I don't feel guilty," she denied, but his glittering look mocked her assertion.

"There's no need to be ashamed of feelings like that," Colter said drily.

"How would you know? You don't have any feelings!" she shot back, unaccountably angered.

"Don't confuse feelings with emotions," he answered in the same level voice as before, not reacting to Natalie's anger. "I see, touch, hear, smell and taste as keenly as the next man. Sexual attraction between opposite sexes is a physical reaction. There is no emotion in desire."

CHAPTER FOUR

A COLD finger ran down her spine, strangely chilled by Colter's detached implication that she might be attracted to Travis McCrea. The carved walnut entrance door stood open and Colter stepped aside for Natalie to precede him.

As she stepped across the threshold, she forced herself to remember that their marriage wasn't real, merely a convenient arrangement. It was clear that Colter had no intention of abiding by the traditions of a bride and groom; to do so would be a mockery. There had been no kiss after the wedding ceremony and now he was letting her walk into her new home instead of carrying her. Thank heaven, there was no need for pretence, she told herself.

Cool, white walls greeted her, accented by dark walnut wood. The floor was tiled in large squares of black and white. Natalie's glimpse of the living room extending out from the foyer promised that the interior of the house was as elegantly casual as the outside. But the main of her attention was focused on the stoutly built, older woman seated on the edge of a straight chair, her hand holding Missy's fingers. Her iron-grey head turned at the sound of their footsteps on the tiles, her blue eyes glinting curious and alert.

"So this is your bride, is it, Colter?" the woman said in a no-nonsense tone as she rose to her feet.

There were few age lines on the woman's face, confined mainly around her eyes and mouth. Her features were stern but, unlike Colter's, her mouth gave the indication that it smiled frequently. It was a strong face and its beauty was in its strength rather than simple prettiness. This was a woman whose friendship was not lightly given.

"Yes, this is my wife Natalie," Colter acknowledged, then introduced the woman to Natalie. "My aunt, Flo Donaldsen."

"How do you do," Natalie smiled. Her hand was enclosed in the woman's firm grip.

"I hope you'll like it here, Mrs. Langston." The tone of Flo Donaldsen's voice said that she doubted it, as her piercing eyes flashed a speaking glance at Colter. "Will you be wanting something to eat?" she asked Colter with distant politeness. "I've already cleared the lunch food, so it wouldn't spoil. You said you would be back this morning."

"That was my fault, Mrs. Donaldsen. I overslept this morning," Natalie spoke up.

"Cake or cookies and something cold will satisfy us until dinner," Colter stated, subtly letting Natalie know there was no need to apologise. "While you're fixing that, I'll show Natalie the bedrooms where she and Ricky will be sleeping. They are prepared?"

There was a silent challenge in his voice, almost daring his aunt to make a personal comment. The woman's mouth tightened fractionally before she replied that they were.

Walking down the corridor on the east wing of the house, Missy shyly pointed out her own bedroom to Natalie and Ricky, a feminine room of saffron yellow and ochre gold flowers. Ricky's room was next to hers, a single bed draped with a red, blue and white print with matching curtains and throw rugs, a distinctly boyish room. But it was the toy train set in the corner that caught his attention, and he impatiently waited while Missy showed him how to operate it.

"Was it yours?" Natalie asked after Colter had suggested they leave the children while he showed her where she would be sleeping.

"Many years ago."

It was difficult for Natalie to picture him as a little boy. She guessed that he had been always

older than his years and not at all the open, embracing child that Ricky was. As Colter opened
the door across the hall from Ricky's, her idle
musings were replaced by admiration. Beautifully crafted oak furniture dominated the room,
its rich patina reflecting the sunny shade of the
avocado and gold area rug. The gold shade was
repeated in the drapes and sheer insets of the
french windows leading out to the portico.

"W-was this your aunt's room?" Natalie
breathed, unable to take her gaze away from the
tasteful furnishings.

"No, she has always used the room off the
kitchen, intended as the maid's or cook's quarters. I was never able to persuade her to take one
of the bedrooms in the main section of the
house once Missy was grown. She insisted that
she wanted her privacy," Colter stated.

"Perhaps I should follow suit," Natalie suggested hesitantly, wanting desperately to enjoy
the luxury of this room while wondering at the
same time whether she was asking too much.
Essentially she was only the housekeeper.

"No, you are my wife. Your place is here in
this room," he returned smoothly. "Besides,
you'll want to be near the boy until he becomes
accustomed to his new surroundings."

"Yes, of course," Natalie agreed, silently
glad that his logic had vanquished her doubts.

"Missy will show you where the dining room is. Flo will have the refreshments out by now." He turned towards the door, expecting Natalie to follow, which she did.

"Aren't you going to join us?"

"I want to check on a few things with Travis."

Natalie hesitated in the hallway, watching Colter as he disappeared in the direction of the foyer. He had been away from the ranch almost an entire week, she reminded herself. Naturally he would be anxious to be brought up to date. She glanced at the other closed doors leading off the hall, wondering which one was his room. It would be austerely masculine like its occupant.

Then the sound of a toy train whistle drew her into Ricky's room. Joining them, she allowed Ricky a few minutes to show her how he could operate the train before she suggested that Missy take them to the dining room. The next item on her agenda after a sweet and a cool drink was to have Mrs. Donaldsen explain the household routine.

At the walnut dining table, Natalie refused the pecan torte Flo Donaldsen offered, choosing to settle for the tall lime cooler. Missy was much less reserved in her great-aunt's company, eagerly responding to her questions about Fiesta, while Ricky began devouring his torte after the first tentative bite. When his plate was clean, he pushed it towards the elderly woman.

"May I have another?" he asked brightly.

"No, Ricky," answered Natalie firmly before Flo Donaldsen had an opportunity to reply. "One is enough."

"Okay," he agreed, not the least bit put out by her refusal as he took a big swallow of the lime drink. "Are you ready, Missy?"

"I have to help Aunt Flo clear the dishes away first," the young girl replied.

"If you don't mind, Missy," Natalie inserted gently, "I'll help her and she can show me where things are in the kitchen. Maybe you could show Ricky around the house and yard?"

Missy hesitated for an instant, glancing at Flo Donaldsen for approval which was given with a slight nod. Excusing herself from the table, she took Ricky's hand and began leading him from the room.

The older woman didn't say a word as they stacked the few dishes and carried them through to the kitchen, a beautifully modern kitchen with every convenience a woman could want. On the counter of the walnut cabinets sat a colander full of squeezed lime halves next to a juicer.

"The limes were fresh?" Natalie murmured in surprise.

"Colter likes his fruits to be fresh." The explanation was given tersely. "He sends a truck to the Rio Grande valley once every two weeks for fruits and vegetables."

"Couldn't he buy them locally?" she asked, blinking her gold-flecked eyes at the extravagance.

"He could," Flo admitted, "but he wants to be sure they're the best."

"That must be expensive." Natalie sat the dishes on the counter by the sink, the full extent of Colter's wealth slowly sinking in.

"He can afford it," the older woman sniffed.

"Yes, I suppose so," Natalie agreed hesitantly.

Youthful blue eyes studied her sharply from an ageing face before the subject was set aside and they stacked the plates and cutlery in the dishwasher. Flo switched it on and then briskly set about explaining the routine of the house.

Wiping the already immaculate dinette table that stood in the middle of the kitchen, Flo concluded, "I've already had most of my things moved to the cottage after Colter telephoned me yesterday. I'll stay at the house tonight to help you with the evening meal and fix breakfast in the morning. After that you're on your own."

Disapproval of their hasty marriage was visible in the rigid lines of the woman's slightly stooped shoulders as she walked to the stove to wipe the top off. Her thick fingers halted their circular movement and she turned to Natalie.

"I know why Colter married you," Flo Donaldsen stated grimly. "When it suits him, he can be very persuasive. I didn't see any love or pretence of love in your eyes when you looked at him. What did you marry him for? Was it his money?"

The blurted questions caught Natalie by surprise. She hadn't expected the older woman to speak so boldly what was on her mind. She stared at her fingers for a moment, studying the plain gold band while the other's sharp gaze watched her in awkward silence.

Tossing her head back proudly, Natalie met the look. "It was a matter of convenience. He needed someone to look after his home and daughter, and Ricky and I needed a home. It wasn't his money nearly as much as it was the promise of some measure of security."

Flo Donaldsen stared at her for more long moments before she breathed in deeply and turned away. "I raised him from a boy. I blamed his father for always reminding him that he was a Langston and different from other people, but I think Colter was naturally born different. He's cold and heartless. You'll live to regret the day you married him."

A chill raced over Natalie's skin as she apprehensively noted the lack of qualification in the woman's statement. There were no "maybes" or "mights". It was a flatly spoken prophecy that held a ring of truth to make it doubly disquieting.

Small fingers tugged impatiently at her hand, demanding her attention. Thrusting aside the woman's pronouncement, Natalie glanced at the boy standing at her side. A smile appeared immediately at the face brimming with happiness.

Colter's approval or affection didn't matter to her. She would be his housekeeper and look after his daughter. Her reward would be in the shining contentment of knowing Ricky would have all the things she wanted to give him—a home, security and a future.

"What is it, Ricky?" Natalie asked patiently.

"Come and look at the swimming pool!" he exclaimed. "There's one in the backyard!"

"I'll be there in a minute. I have to help Mrs. Donaldsen first."

"Run along," the woman spoke up. "I'll be starting dinner around five. You can come and help me then."

"Please, you have to see it," Ricky insisted.

"All right." Natalie gave in laughingly, unable to deny the entreaty of those sparkling brown eyes.

The front of the house had only hinted at the beauty to be found in the rear gardens. Honeysuckle vines covered the rock walls, their sweet fragrance mingling with other heady scents. The scarlet pinks of oleander blossoms coated their bush home while the more delicate dusty pink of the mimosa tree dotted its branches. At the end of the walled enclosure was a swimming pool, its smooth waters reflecting the vivid blue of the sky.

A slatted bench swing was firmly suspended from the thick branch of an oak. Natalie couldn't resist its lure and Ricky scrambled up to sit beside her, soon joined by Missy. Listening with half an ear to Ricky's chatter, Natalie drank in the tropical serenity of the garden, inwardly laughing at the thought of ever regretting the events that brought her here.

The relative inactivity of the swing soon palled for Ricky, and Missy obligingly produced a large beach ball for a lively game of catch while Natalie looked on. Relaxed, her worries gone, she didn't notice the increasing length of the shadows until she accidentally glanced at her watch and saw the hands pointing to half past four.

With a start of surprise at the quick flight of time, Natalie slipped out of the swing, calling to Missy and Ricky that she was going into the house to help Mrs. Donaldsen prepare dinner. As she stepped through the french doors into the living room, she heard the sound of a car speeding into the driveway. Immediately there was the strident blare of the horn. Curiosity impelled Natalie across the room to the windows looking out to the front entrance.

Pushing the ivory sheer curtains aside, she saw Colter and Travis McCrea approaching the house through the trees. A dust cloud was just settling over the dark green foreign sports car that had ground to a halt in the drive. A woman with long, shimmering curls of red-gold emerged from the car, scantily clad in an emerald green midriff top and white slacks that rested on her hip-bones.

The thick walls of the house made her words of greeting indistinguishable to Natalie, but she was left in little doubt as to whom they were meant for as the attractive, curvaceous redhead glided over the ground to Colter.

Natalie breathed in sharply in disgust when the woman didn't stop but continued her slow deliberate movements that first had her hands touch Colter's chest as her head tilted back to smile. But she didn't stop there. Her hands twined themselves about his neck while she suggestively and openly pressed her body against Colter's. His mouth was quirked derisively at the corners before it was pulled down to be claimed in an obviously passion-filled kiss.

Natalie's blood ran cold at the sight of Colter's hands resting lightly on the bare flesh of the woman's waist. His complete lack of resistance kindled a fiery rage that didn't ease when his head rose slowly from the woman's kiss. Not until she saw his gaze turn towards the house did Natalie let the curtain fall into place, suddenly aware that if Colter hadn't seen her at the window, Travis McCrea had.

She trembled with a frustrated kind of fury. If Colter had married her to stop the gossip that would have come if she had merely lived in his home as a housekeeper, then surely she was entitled to some respect from him as his wife.

Then she brought herself up sharply. That hadn't been his reason for marrying her. He had married her to be certain she wouldn't be free to leave whenever she chose. There had been no mention that there would be any pretence of a real marriage between them.

Her stomach lurched with sickening swiftness as Natalie realised that whatever women Colter knew, he would go on knowing. His very action at not attempting to forestall the woman's embrace with Travis looking on proved that he didn't care if Natalie became an object of ridicule.

It was a jolting discovery, a serpent in the garden of Eden. Her assumption that as his wife she was entitled to an outward show of his respect had been misplaced.

Her self-derisive thoughts were so loud Natalie didn't hear the car churning out of the gravelled drive. The opening and closing of the front door alerted her to the fact that she was still standing with her back to the window. Too late to move, she lifted her head in proud defiance, preparing to reject the pity that Travis's brown eyes would offer. But Colter walked into the living room alone, aloof, strikingly handsome, and arrogant, the adjectives that described him so accurately. His gaze flicked from Natalie to the window, then back to her face.

"Deirdre decided against staying." His mouth moved into a humourless smile as he walked lithely into the room.

The smoothness with which he spoke the name of the girl he had just been kissing sent freezing ripples of anger through Natalie's veins. Yellow flames blazed in her eyes.

"Deirdre?" Her brow arched in haughty question, determined to show him she was not a doormat to be walked on.

"Deirdre Collins, the daughter of one of the neighbouring ranchers," Colter elucidated, stopping calmly in front of her.

Unwittingly Natalie's gaze was drawn to the hard line of his mouth, seeking traces of lipstick. "More than a neighbour's daughter, surely," she mocked.

Her cutting barb seemed only to amuse him. "I believe she considered herself to be," he agreed.

Again she was sharply reminded of his coldness, his lack of compassion for another human's feelings. She averted her gaze from the glittering mockery of his.

"Where's Travis? I thought he was with you," she said coldly.

"I believe he was under the impression that you might be embarrassed." Derisive laughter edged his voice.

"Because I saw you kissing that woman?" Her shoulders moved in an uncaring shrug, as if the scene hadn't concerned her in the least.

"Actually I was being kissed rather than the other way around," corrected Colter with infuriating evenness.

"You were hardly protesting!" Natalie snapped, and immediately turned away, trembling with rage.

"Does that bother you?"

"Of course not!" she denied, trying to ignore the eyes boring into her rigid shoulders.

"Then why are you angry?"

Natalie was tempted to tell him that she wasn't, but she had already made the contrary clear. Tightening her fingers into impotent fists at her side, she turned back to him, subduing her temper to reply in an unruffled tone.

"I hadn't realised that you intended to broadcast the fact that I was nothing more than a glorified housekeeper and babysitter, undeserving of any degree of respect from you as your wife."

"Do you mean you want us to pretend that we care for each other?" he jeered, revealing his contempt for the idea. "To display affection for each other to outside eyes?"

"No, I don't mean that at all!" Natalie denied vigorously. "I simply don't want to be held up to ridicule in the community where Ricky has to grow up."

"Legally bearing my name will bring you a great deal of respect," Colter stated.

Her mouth tightened into a mutinous line. "And make me the subject of a lot of gossip," she added.

"Do you care what people say?"

"Only if it hurts Ricky."

"Do you feel neglected and insulted because I haven't kissed you yet, though I remarked once that you were desirable?" Colter inquired, a disquieting glitter in the eyes that roamed her face.

"I've already told you what I expect, and that's respect. Nothing more." Her nerves suddenly vibrated at how very close he was standing to her, so virilely masculine, so sinuously strong.

"Do you mean you didn't expect to be the first woman I kissed after we were married?" His mocking amusement was unmistakable.

His finger touched the heightened colour in her cheek when Natalie flushed at the remembrance that she had expected a duty kiss after the wedding ceremony, a meaningless kiss to keep up appearances. She pressed her lips tightly shut rather than admit that. Glaring at his coldly remote blue-green eyes, she remained immobile under the caressing touch of his finger along her cheek and jaw, determined to show her complete indifference to him, an indifference that was equal to his.

"Perhaps I should correct that deficiency."

The words were barely spoken and his hand was closing firmly over her chin. Her eyes widened in surprise as her hands came up to his chest to push him away. But the attempt was wasted motion as his arm swept around her to check the movement away from him.

The swiftness of his action was only implied and Natalie was aware of the slow deliberation that controlled Colter. When the hard line of his mouth began its descent to hers, she didn't attempt to struggle. Impassive submission was the best deterrent for an unwanted kiss.

The touch of his mouth drew an involuntary and tiny gasp of surprise. His coldness, remoteness, his lack of emotion had not prepared her for the warm, mobile pressure of his kiss. Natalie had expected his lovemaking to be forceful, even cruel, but certainly not this seductive mastery that coerced response. An enveloping warmth swept through her body as his hand slipped from her chin to the vulnerable curve of her throat.

His expertise was beyond her experience and she reeled from the shock of it when his head rose from hers. Had she kissed him in return? she wondered dazedly as she blinked at the unchanging mask of his aristocratic face. The betraying shudders within said that she had, although Natalie had no recollection of doing so. The predominantly green light in his eyes seemed to indicate an arrogant satisfaction as Colter examined the parted fullness of her lips, still trembling from the firm imprint of his mouth. The light didn't vary when it slid to hold her gaze.

"It's been a long time since you have been kissed, hasn't it?" he inquired, relaxing his hold on her throat and back so she could move away.

"Yes."

From somewhere she dredged up the strength to reply, seizing on the thought as the reason that his kiss had inexplicably moved her. She had never been a prude. A man's kiss had always been pleasurable if not exciting.

"That's a pity," Colter drawled lazily. Indifference was again drawn in his starkly handsome face, like a mountain cat tired of its prey after the first taste of blood. "You might be quite good with a little more experience."

Natalie sputtered indignantly before realising that her temper was wasted on Colter. He had already released her and stepped away, a lit cigarette between the lips that had just awoken her senses to his masculinity.

Spinning abruptly on her heel, she started for the kitchen, tossing over her shoulder, "I'm going to help Mrs. Donaldsen fix dinner."

"Where's Missy and the boy?"

"Ricky," her teeth grated in anger as Natalie emphasised her nephew's name, "and Missy are playing ball in the back."

Flo Donaldsen was all briskness and efficiency when Natalie arrived in the kitchen, instructing her first in the arrangement of items in the well-stocked cupboards. While Natalie prepared a fresh pineapple, the older woman started cutting thick portions of ham to be broiled as steaks with the pineapple rings.

If she noticed the glow that was still in Natalie's cheeks, she didn't refer to it, her comments on the advisability of their marriage already made. And Natalie was too eager to show Colter's aunt that she was not a novice in the kitchen to allow her mind to wander back to the disturbing kiss.

As Natalie began collecting the plates and glasses to set the dining room table, Flo Donaldsen said, "I had Juan—he's the handyman and gardener—take your suitcases up to your rooms. I would have unpacked them for you, but I thought you'd rather do that yourself later tonight."

"Thank you," Natalie responded, silently wondering if the woman wasn't insinuating that she and Ricky would be better off to leave them packed. Shaking away that impression, she chose to add a less personal comment. "The gardens and the house are very beautifully kept."

"Hummph," Flo sniffed, lifting the lid of one of the pans on the stove to check the vegetables being steamed. " 'Stone walls do not a prison make'."

Glancing at the older woman apprehensively, Natalie decided to ignore the remark. She could hardly regard herself as a prisoner in this house. Her presence here was the result of her own free will, the decision made with a full understanding of the relative permanency of her position in the home, at least until Ricky was grown.

The first meal in her new home was a successful one, successful from the standpoint that the food was deliciously prepared and the company was pleasant. Travis McCrea dominated the conversation with his easy confident charm, not at all obtrusive, with Ricky occasionally competing for control of the subject matter.

For the most part, Travis kept the conversation channelled to the events of Fiesta week in San Antonio, drawing out Missy's shy observations on the activities and chuckling at Ricky's bolder statements. Travis kept the talk away from personal inquiries into Natalie's life or the way she had met Colter.

Colter did not remain totally silent, but mostly he observed, his comments generally restricted to Ricky's questions about the ranch.

He seemed to be prepared for Ricky's interest, and Natalie silently wondered how long his apparent patience would last under Ricky's insatiable curiosity.

When the dinner dishes were cleared and the strawberry dessert placed on the table, Ricky leaned forward to look past Natalie at Colter seated at the head of the table.

"Will you take me to see the cows and horses tomorrow?" he asked, but it was closer to a demand. "Missy wouldn't take me to see them today. She said we weren't allowed down there."

"Ricky!" Natalie said in a shushing tone, certain this time that he had trespassed too far by asking Colter to give him a tour of the ranch. "Mr.—" A sideways glance at the light brown head saw eyebrow-arching mockery at her almost formal reference to the man who was her husband. "Colter," she corrected quickly, feeling the warmth climbing up her neck, "will be too busy tomorrow to show you around."

"Will you?" Ricky asked, wanting to hear it from Colter's lips, ignoring Natalie's frown to be silent.

"I probably will tomorrow," Colter agreed, "but maybe the day after. We'll see."

"Can I ride a horse?" Satisfied with his half-promise, Ricky pursued another tangent.

There was a trace of exasperation in Natalie's sigh that brought an amused glance from Travis McCrea's rugged face seated across the table from her.

"Have you ever ridden a horse before?" Colter asked him, not missing the smiling exchange between his wife and his foreman yet totally unconcerned by it.

"No," Ricky admitted as if it was of little consequence to his request.

"Have you?" The compelling blue-green gaze was turned to Natalie.

"Some years ago but I'm hardly experienced," she replied.

"Pick out some suitable mounts for them," he instructed Travis.

"I think I know just the pair," the dark-haired man nodded, winking at Ricky, who was beside himself with glee.

"Do you ride, Missy?" Natalie asked, trying to include the young girl so she wouldn't feel left out of the activities.

A nervous glance was darted at her father, who responded for her. "She used to ride. She was thrown from a horse two years ago and dislocated her hip. She hasn't been on a horse since then."

Missy crimsoned at the detached criticism in

Colter's reply. Natalie felt her heart reaching out to the young girl in sympathy. Fear was an awesome thing. Missy was not naturally adventurous, which only increased fear's hold.

CHAPTER FIVE

COFFEE FOLLOWED dessert for the adults while Ricky and Missy excused themselves from the table to enjoy the last of the sunlight outdoors.

A scarlet-orange disc was hovering over the treetops when Natalie finished helping Mrs. Donaldsen with the last of the dinner dishes and went in search of Ricky. There was a halfhearted assertion that he wasn't tired, but a yawn accompanied his statement and Ricky followed Natalie to his bedroom.

There was a bathroom situated in the hallway between his room and Missy's. While Ricky bathed, Natalie unpacked his cases, barely filling the empty drawers of the dressing-table and the roomy closet. She was just turning back the covers of his bed when he padded into the room.

"Will you read me a story? I washed real good." He held out his small hands for her inspection.

Long, curling lashes fluttered down to conceal bright brown eyes long before the Three Bears discovered Goldilocks in their home.

Natalie tucked the bedcovers tightly about him, brushed a kiss to the forehead covered with silky brown hair and tiptoed out of his room, leaving the door slightly ajar in case he called for her in the night.

Before Natalie returned to her own room, she looked in on Missy. She was sitting in bed with a book propped on her knees. Her nondescript brown hair was free of its braid, flowing down her shoulders to her waist in crisp waves. Its length made the young girl's face look longer and thinner. Natalie silently resolved to persuade Missy to have her hair cut into a shorter style some future time when they were better acquainted.

"I stopped in to wish you a good night," Natalie smiled.

"Is Ricky in bed?" Missy asked.

"In bed and already sound asleep, and he wasn't tired," she laughed softly, and received an answering smile of understanding at Ricky's initial reluctance to go to bed.

Then the smile faded from Missy's face as she darted a shy look at Natalie. "I'm . . . I'm glad you and Ricky came to live with us," she offered hesitatingly.

"So am I," Natalie nodded calmly, knowing this was not the time to grasp too firmly at Missy's tentative hand of friendship. "Good night, Missy, and have a nice night."

"Good night—Natalie."

As Natalie opened the door to her room, there was a satisfied gleam in her eyes. Ricky was adapting easily, as only a child can, to his new life, and Missy was on the verge of accepting them both completely and without reservation. The future seemed to hold a very rosy glow.

Her suitcases stood at the foot of the bed. As she approached them to begin her own unpacking, she spied the door, to what she had thought was a closet, standing ajar. The glimpse of lush carpet and shining porcelain revealed that it was not a closet.

Curious, Natalie stepped through the open doorway, gazing with pleasure at the spacious private bath. Contrasting the three white walls, the fourth was covered with a mural of a green landscape. But the most striking feature of the bathroom was the sunken tub, luxuriously deep and large.

Thick bath towels hung on a gold rack. A glass shelf near the tub held a dish of yellow-gold soap in the shape of rosebuds. Beside it was an unopened container of lavender-scented bath salts, no doubt a peace offering from Mrs. Donaldsen.

The prospect of lazing in the sunken tub filled with fragrant bubbles was infinitely more inviting than unpacking the suitcases in the adjoining room. And, Natalie told herself, she could always unpack after a relaxing bath.

Thus convinced, she turned on the gold taps and adjusted the water temperature, liberally adding the lavender-scented salts. In her bedroom, she shook out the gold lounging robe from the smaller of the two suitcases and carried it and the cosmetic case into the bathroom.

Nearly three-quarters of an hour later, Natalie stood in front of the vanity mirror above the gleaming porcelain sink, feeling clean and refreshed and blissfully feminine. Fluffing the ends of her shining honey-brown hair with a comb, she tried to recall the last time she had felt free to spend so much time on herself. It seemed very long ago.

The cowled neckline of her robe curled in a wide circle about her neck, revealing the delicate hollows of her collarbones and the graceful curve of her throat. The muted gold shade intensified the sparkling amber lights in her hazel eyes. Her features were no longer etched with worry and tension, but soft and alluringly beautiful with her new-found security. With the pinched look of strain gone, Natalie didn't look nearly so thin.

With a satisfied smile turning up the corners of her mouth, she switched off the bathroom light and walked back into her bedroom.

Her expression froze at the sight of Colter standing near the bed in the act of tossing his shirt on the chair.

"What are you doing in here?" Natalie demanded in a less than commanding tone as she stared in disbelief at the leanly muscular and naked chest.

He spared her a sliding glance of unconcern as he unbuckled his belt and slipped it from the waistband of his trousers. "Getting ready for bed."

"But . . . but this is my room," she faltered, her heart beating wildly.

"Yes, it's your room, too," Colter agreed, emptying his pockets on to the dressing-table top.

"Too?" she echoed weakly, still in the grip of surprise. "But I thought—"

Colter turned slowly, his dispassionate face examining her startled expression. "What exactly did you think?"

Natalie whirled away from his compelling gaze, her hand clutching the zippered front of her robe. Striving to achieve a calmness she was far from feeling, she breathed in deeply. The short burst of derisive laughter that followed her movement nearly brought back the sense of panic.

"You didn't honestly believe this was going to be one of those 'in-name-only' marriages, did you?" Colter jeered.

Her temper flared instantly at his cynical tone. "Last night—" she began indignantly.

But he interrupted with cutting swiftness. "Last night accommodation with suitable privacy couldn't be arranged."

"You may as well know now that I have no intention of going to bed with you." Natalie tilted her head to a defiant angle. "We may have gone through the formalities of a marriage ceremony, but we are not truly man and wife."

"Not yet," qualified Colter, his hands resting complacently on his hips.

"Not ever!" she flashed, spinning away from the unmistakably masculine figure to seek some place of safety.

With the swiftness of the cougar she had likened him to, Colter had a steel grip on her arm and was jerking her rigid body around to face him. His narrowed gaze raked her face with its look of outrage.

"Did you honestly expect to live in this house the dozen or so years before Ricky is grown without ever once having me touch you?" His other hand closed suggestively over her hip bone and pulled her against the taut muscles of his thighs. "I'm a man, Natalie. The urge to possess a desirable and attractive woman like you is natural and I have no intention of denying it."

Natalie had no idea what she had thought, if she had even given it a thought. She stiffly maintained the pressure against his hold, glaring at him coldly.

"I'm not a slave to be taken whenever the mood strikes you," she stated sharply. "You may have provided me and Ricky with a home and security. I'm grateful for that, but not even gratitude will make me submit to you. No one has ever touched me, and if you try, I'll scream."

"And who will hear you?" Colter whispered softly, but with an undercurrent of derision. "Flo is on the other side of the house, no doubt fast asleep, and her hearing isn't as keen as it once was. Your voice wouldn't carry to the quarters of the ranch hands. The only ones that would hear your cries would be Ricky and Missy."

Natalie paled at the undeniable truth of his words. Fear took the edge from her anger as she frantically examined his aloof expression for some sign of compassion or mercy. Nothing. The only thing that gave her hope was the lack of desire burning in his eyes. She had seen the look that came into men's eyes when they wanted to make love to a girl, and it was noticeably absent in Colter's.

"You don't want me," she asserted breathlessly.

His hold on her arm and hip didn't slacken. "It's just as well that I'm not ruled by passion," the hard line of his mouth moved into a mirthless smile, "if, as you say, no man has ever touched you before."

She gasped sharply as waves of panic assailed her. With her free hand, she tried to push herself away from his chest, to struggle free, but his strength was far superior to hers. He crushed her against him, almost denying her breath.

"If you fight me, I'll have to be rough," he growled near her ear. "If you'll let me, I'll be gentle."

The roar of blood in her ears seemed to deprive the rest of her body of its strength. With the iron band of his arms pressing her against him, Natalie felt the nakedness of his skin burning through her robe, singeing her nerve ends until she felt nothing but him. She bent her head back, as far away from the hard chest as his hold would permit.

Fear and loathing glittered in her eyes that stared into his darkly tanned and impassive face, ruthlessly set with the implacability of his intent. Breath came in tiny gasps for air through parted lips.

"How can you do this when you know I'm not willing?" Natalie demanded, knowing her protest was useless, but refusing to submit like some passive slave.

Frosty blue-green eyes travelled lazily over her upturned face. "I mean this marriage to begin as I intend it to go on."

As she twisted her head away, Colter shifted his hold, pinning both arms behind her back in the grip of one hand. His free hand moved to her throat, the touch against her skin sending convulsive shudders quivering through her. Foolishly Natalie didn't guess his intention until she felt the zipper of her robe opening against her skin.

"No!" The word was torn from her throat in breathless panic.

She struggled desperately to impede the zipper's progress, succeeding only to a limited extent. With her bare foot she kicked at his shins. A wince of pain flashed across his face, but Colter didn't lessen his hold. Instead he swung her off her feet into his arms and carried her to the bed, dumping her on to the exposed sheets like a sack of potatoes.

Before Natalie could recover and slide off the opposite side, the overhead light was switched off and the weight of his body was on the mattress beside her, his hands instinctively finding her in the dark.

With all the power at her command, she fought him off, kicking and clawing at him like a wild thing. Occasionally she felt the warm wetness of blood where her nails had made their mark on his shoulders and back. Her frantic violence only sapped her energy, leaving her exhausted and weak on the bed, her arms stretched above her head by Colter's hands, her robe tossed somewhere on the floor.

A moment to catch her breath, that was all she needed, she told herself, and stiffened as she felt the warmth of his mouth on the cord of her neck. During all her struggles, he had not touched her, only warding off her flailing arms and legs and keeping her on the bed beside him. Her robe had been stripped from her, but the hands that did it had not been interested in the bareness beneath it.

Weakly Natalie tried to pull her wrists from his hands and twist her body free of the pinning weight of his chest. Her attempts were pathetic and she knew it.

"Stop fighting," Colter ordered quietly. "You'll only hurt yourself."

"And you won't?" she hissed bitterly.

Her mistake was in turning her head to glare at him. Immediately his mouth took possession of hers, branding his ownership with burning thoroughness. At some point in the provocative mastery of his kisses, a whirling void opened up and Natalie was pulled into the burning blackness.

It was much later before Colter rolled away from her, not leaving until he had drawn an involuntary gasp of pleasure from her lips. For interminable seconds, Natalie lay weak and spent where he had left her, struggling to surface from the fiery sensations that swamped her consciousness.

In one part of her mind there was nothing but loathing for the man who had truly become her husband. The rest was still reeling from the sensual shock of his lovemaking, its aftermath not as unpleasant as she wanted it to be.

Rolling on to her side, she was filled with self-disgust at the admission, despising herself as much as she loathed Colter. If tears could have erased the memory, she would have cried. Instead she curled into a tight ball of misery.

The moon had risen above the treetops. Its light was streaming through the sheer curtains at the window, laying a silvery path across the bed. The droning song of the cicadas sounded in the distance, punctuated by the call of the bullfrogs, and a night bird trilled to the stars. The world should have stopped, but it hadn't.

"You'll live to regret the day you married him," Flo Donaldsen's words came flying to her mind.

Fiesta. Natalie had married Colter on the last day of Fiesta San Antonio, a celebration of independence. Imprudently she had not guessed he intended to use her to satisfy all his needs. The gold band on her finger was a symbol of ownership and Natalie didn't intend to be a slave. If she and Ricky had to walk all the way back to San Antonio, she would not stay in this house another night.

"Natalie."

Colter's fingers closed over her arm as he spoke. His tone was detached and impersonal, disregarding the complete intimacy they had shared only moments ago.

A shiver of sensual awareness danced over her skin, igniting an answering spark within her. The involuntary response of her body angered Natalie and she wrenched her arm free of his touch.

"Leave me alone," she demanded tautly.

His reply was a punishing grip on her shoulder that pushed it back on to the sheet and held her flat. There was no more reason to fight, so

Natalie lay in rigid unresistance, keeping her head turned away from him.

"Look at me," he commanded. When she didn't comply, Colter took hold of her chin and twisted her face to his. "I said look at me," he repeated in a firmly relentless voice as she kept her gaze averted.

Resentment flamed brightly when Natalie focused her gaze on his face, moonlight shimmering white-gold on the sun-bleached hair falling across the smooth forehead. Metallic chips of blue steel looked back at her, immune to the loathing in her eyes.

"Don't touch me," Natalie ordered contemptuously.

A brow flicked upward in cynical mockery while his other hand slid over her silken skin to the swell of her breast, effectively reminding her that she was not the one to give orders. Natalie breathed in sharply, but didn't draw away. It would have been useless.

"I know what you're thinking," Colter stated evenly.

"Do you?" she jeered.

"You're thinking about running away," he answered. Her brown lashes fluttered slightly in surprise, but there was no other admission in her expression that his guess was anywhere near accurate. "Where would you go? You can't go back to your apartment because you know I'll follow. You don't have any money to get a new one. Without a job, how do you intend to support yourself and Ricky? Or were you planning to leave Ricky here?''

"Of course not," Natalie retorted. Her teeth sank into her lower lip, too late to bite back her words of admission.

"What would you accomplish by running?" Natalie refused to reply to the quiet mockery of his question. "Would it change what happened tonight? Would you be able to forget that it ever happened?"

He knew the answers to his questions before he asked them and she closed her eyes tightly to avoid seeing the truth he was trying to force her to admit.

"Little has changed," continued Colter. "You still have the security you wanted for you and the boy, the freedom from want, a decent home and clothing."

"But look at the price I had to pay." This time her voice was choked with emotion, her eyes still closed to shut out the image of his handsome face—only to have her mind's eye visualise it.

"Women of your age are rarely virgins," he mocked. "It isn't my fault that you were. And

it was something I couldn't know until tonight."

"It's your fault that I'm not now!" Natalie
flared.

"Did you intend to remain inviolate the rest
of your life?" The mouth that had aroused her
desire curled into a derisive smile. "Or did you
think to take a lover at a future time while you
denied your husband his marriage bed?"

"I didn't think about it at all." Her reply was
truthful.

She had been too relieved at having Ricky's
future secured and the responsibility lightened
on herself to consider her own personal future.
Colter's own indifference had lulled her into
believing the physical aspect of their marriage
was not important.

"We're married. That's a fact you can't ignore," Colter reminded her.

"And you don't intend to let me forget it,"
Natalie responded bitterly.

"No, I don't," he agreed. His pinning grip
relaxed. "So stop forcing a hysterical reaction
that you don't feel. We both know it wasn't an
experience totally without pleasure for you.
There's no reason to pretend that it was. Leaving here would accomplish nothing and change
nothing. Go to sleep, Natalie, and let someone

who's a more convincing actress play the role of the outraged female.''

In the next instant she was free of his hold and his touch, trembling with an urge to strike out at him as he lay beside her. She suppressed it, knowing that Colter would not think twice about retaliating. She rolled on to her side away from his long length, curling her arms about the pillow and hugging it tightly to her.

Sleep was nearly immediate, denying Natalie the opportunity to consider what her alternatives were. There was not another conscious thought until morning when she became aware of the sunlight trying to shine through her closed eyes and the sensation that someone else was in the room with her.

The events of the night before came racing back and her eyelids sprang open, her gaze focusing on the empty pillow beside her.

''So you're finally awake,'' but it was a woman's voice that spoke from the side of the room and not Colter's as Natalie had anticipated.

At the sight of Flo Donaldsen, Natalie pushed herself into a nearly upright position in the bed, dragging the covers with her. A telltale warmth invaded her face and she raised a hand to brush the hair away from her face to conceal her self-consciousness for a moment from the woman's sharp gaze.

"What time is it?" asked Natalie.

"Nearly ten. Colter left orders to let you sleep this morning," Flo added in explanation. "But I thought you'd want a chance to shower and dress before lunchtime. I'll be staying on to fix it, so you needn't worry about that."

"Thank you," Natalie murmured as her gaze slid away from the woman's discerning face only to rush back a second later. "Where's Ricky?"

"Colter took him along this morning. Would you be wanting anything for breakfast?"

"No, just coffee."

Flo Donaldsen nodded and left the room. There was a slight protest of her muscles as Natalie slipped from the bed and hurried into the bathroom, needing the cleansing waters of a bath in order to face the day ahead of her.

Her mouth had tightened into a grim line at Flo's pronouncement that Ricky was with Colter. Though she did not yet know Colter thoroughly, she knew consideration was not the motive for his action. He had known she wouldn't leave without Ricky.

He always seemed to be one step ahead of her. Even letting her sleep late had been a means of ensuring that his aunt was aware they had slept together.

After bathing and dressing, Natalie stripped the sheets from the bed, put on fresh ones from the linen closet in the hallway that Missy had pointed out the previous day. Then she made her way to the kitchen where Flo Donaldsen was fixing lunch. Natalie was setting the dining table when Ricky came bursting through the front door.

"Nonnie! Nonnie!" he cried excitedly as he rushed towards her.

Automatically she knelt to receive his quick hug and remained in the same position to be nearer to his level. Her loving smile was automatic and genuine as she looked into his snapping brown eyes, sparkling with immeasurable happiness.

"Oh, Nonnie! You should have been with us!" he exclaimed. "I got to see the horses and barns and pet a dog and everything! And C-Colter," he glanced over his shoulder as he struggled momentarily with the name, "is going to take me out to see the cows and their babies this afternoon," Ricky concluded gleefully.

Natalie's gaze swept past Ricky to the man standing in the archway of the dining room, blue-green eyes holding her gaze. Colter's lazy yet alert study of her sent the blood pounding through her veins, anger seething at the selfish way he was using Ricky to ensure that the boy would be against any suggestion that they leave the ranch.

"The boy can come," Colter qualified amicably as he stepped farther into the room, "providing you don't have any objections."

"I can, can't I?" Ricky pleaded.

Natalie glared at Colter. "Would my objections matter?" she taunted.

His gaze narrowed, the colour of his eyes shifting to a harsher shade of blue, frosty and cold. "If you've made other plans, then say so."

Deliberately Natalie ignored his challenge as she flashed a tense smile at the small boy standing in front of her. "Go and wash your hands, Ricky. We'll talk about it after lunch."

He hesitated as if to argue for immediate permission, then scampered away. Natalie straightened stiffly, her head drawn back to a defiant angle.

"You don't play fair," she accused in an ominous undertone.

"I don't 'play' at anything," Colter returned.

Involuntarily her voice rose. "You know very well what I mean! Every little boy dreams of being a cowboy, and you're deliberately making sure that Ricky realises that his dream can come true if we stay here."

"Is there some question that you will?" There was an arrogant lift of his eyebrow.

A stabbing pain jabbed at her chest as Natalie realised that she inwardly had accepted the situation. It was a disturbing discovery to acknowledge that all her protests were only bold talk that she had no intention of backing up with action. She was ashamed of her helplessness, the lack of strength that had prompted her to accept his offer of marriage without giving any thought to the consequences.

Despite Colter's insensitivity, he was strong. In the short time she had known him, Natalie had learned what it was like to have a man to rely on, to make the decisions. So while she cursed her weakness, she resolved not to reveal it to Colter. Let him think that some day she might leave, she told herself, and some day she would find the strength to do it.

He was still waiting for her answer, his alertness more pronounced than ever at her silence. There was satisfaction in realising he was not entirely certain of her reaction. Gold dust sparkled in her almond eyes as she met his searching look. Without replying Natalie turned away, a mysterious smile flitting over her mouth.

"I want an answer," Colter stated.

When Natalie failed to answer and started to walk away, his fingers closed over her arm and spun her around.

The hard pressure of his hand was like a catalyst, suddenly causing a rush of vivid memories, recalling the way he had caressed her so intimately the night before and her own instinctive reaction to his touch.

Immediately she tried to pull free of his hold, hissing angrily, "Don't touch me!"

When she failed to pull free, her other hand raised to strike a lean cheek and the taunting curve of his mouth. But its movement was halted in mid-swing by the vice-like grip of his hand and Natalie was twisted against his muscular length, her breath stolen by the sudden contact.

"You're a disgusting animal!" she spat softly, and drew a short derisive laugh from Colter.

"And you're a wildcat." His eyes mockingly inspected her face. "I enjoyed taming you last night."

The instant of immobility at the hard pressure of his body against her was gone, chased away by his jeering comment. Although knowing it was futile, Natalie struggled against his hold anyway.

"Let me go!" she demanded hoarsely. "I despise you. I don't want you to touch me!"

The last vibrated in the air. There was a movement behind Colter and for a frightened second Natalie thought it was Ricky witnessing their argument. Then her face flamed in embarrassment when she saw Travis McCrea, his brows drawn together in a concerned frown. She sensed his indecision, uncertain whether to step forward and interfere or to leave before his presence was noticed.

Colter turned his head to see the reason for her disconcerted expression. Natalie glanced tensely at his almost impassive face, noting the narrowing of his gaze as Colter dared Travis to intervene. Then her look slid back to Travis, the frown gone, a humourless smile curving the mouth that had been grim.

"Your first argument, huh?" Travis inserted casually as he walked into the dining room. "I've heard that's always the first sign that the honeymoon is over."

Accepting Travis's observation, Colter studied Natalie's averted face, its colour only just beginning to return to normal.

"Do you wish you could run home to Mama?" he jeered, lowering his voice to a pitch that wouldn't carry his words to Travis's hearing.

There was no sign that the dark, rugged foreman had heard his question. As Colter's hold
on her arms slackened, Natalie pulled away, ignoring his jibe and murmuring self-consciously,
"I have to help Mrs. Donaldsen." A faltering
excuse, but the only one she had.

CHAPTER SIX

STRANGELY LIFE fell into a comfortable pattern for Natalie. Although her pride demanded that she pretend otherwise, the undemanding routine of cleaning house, taking care of Missy and Ricky, and preparing meals was truly enjoyable. She had never been career-minded, always desiring a home and family. Now that she had both, there was a sense of fulfilment that more ambitious members of her sex would never understand.

Not that everything had gone smoothly. Initially there had been confusion when Flo Donaldsen had departed for her cottage, but Natalie had soon found her way around. And there had been the task of enrolling Ricky in the afternoon kindergarten class at the local school for the rest of the term.

Colter gave her almost free rein, providing her with keys to the El Dorado, giving her a list of the stores he had accounts with, and generally letting her do as she pleased as long as she maintained their bargain.

During the day, Natalie never had to suffer his company alone, since he only appeared at mealtimes and then in the company of Travis McCrea. In the evenings he was in the house most of the time, but those were the hours she spent with Ricky and Missy. Colter never requested her company nor indicated a desire to establish a more companionable relationship between them.

When they were alone, Natalie didn't hesitate to let her distaste of him show, but the sensuous warmth of his kisses always produced a reaction that was purely physical and out of the bounds of her control.

Natalie had just returned the vacuum cleaner to the utility closet when she heard the front door open and close. She glanced swiftly at her wristwatch, wondering if she had lost track of time and Missy and Ricky were home from school.

But it wasn't nearly time for them, so she moved curiously to the living room. Her steps halted abruptly at the sight of the vivacious redhead wandering familiarly about the room. It was the woman Colter had identified as Deirdre Collins who had thrown herself into his arms the first day Natalie had arrived at the ranch.

"May I help you?" Natalie inquired, knowing her face and voice were stiff and cold, and not caring.

The redhead turned, a haughty look to her green eyes as she openly surveyed Natalie. Poise, sophistication and wealth were stamped in the clothes and hairstyle that the strikingly beautiful woman wore. In spite of herself, Natalie thrust her chin to a slightly more defiant angle. The action drew an immediate smile of satisfaction to the perfect copper lips.

"You're the new Mrs. Langston, of course," the redhead murmured with brittle friendliness. "I'm Deirdre Collins. I wanted to meet you and offer my congratulations. I hope you don't mind me barging in this way." A manicured hand waved the air in apology. "I'm used to coming and going as I please. It never occurred to me until just now that Colter might not have mentioned me."

"Yes, he has. Your parents are our neighbours, aren't they?" said Natalie. Her temper was slowly reaching the boiling point, increased by Deirdre Collins's patronising attitude. "As a matter of fact," she added boldly, "I believe you were here the first day Colter and I returned after we were married. I'm sorry I didn't get to meet you then."

The woman's gaze narrowed slightly as she met the flashing amber caution lights in Natalie's eyes. "I hope," Deirdre hesitated, obviously choosing her words carefully, "my appearance that day didn't upset you."

"Not in the least. After all, you weren't aware that Colter was married," she returned with the same caustic edge to her voice.

Deirdre stared at Natalie for a long moment before swinging her emerald gaze around the room. "Colter has a beautiful home, doesn't he? Are you the domesticated type?" The sarcasm gleamed out through a see-through veil.

"Yes, I am," Natalie admitted without any apology.

"I loathe the routine of a house myself. I would make a lousy wife." Again a smile curved the copper mouth. "Besides, a wife always gets taken for granted. I'd rather have a man waiting on me, seeking my favours, rather than the other way around. No man should see a woman when she first gets up in the morning. It destroys his illusions."

Natalie knew exactly what Deirdre was hinting at and she realised that she had unconsciously known all along that Deirdre had probably been Colter's mistress. But was she insinuating something more? That she still was?

Colter could have a dozen mistresses for all Natalie cared, but if he thought she was going to welcome them into her home—and it was her home—then he was in for a rude awakening.

"I'm sorry Colter isn't here, Miss Collins. I know he'll regret missing your visit." As tactfully as possible Natalie was suggesting that Deirdre leave. Under no circumstances was she going to offer the redhead any refreshments.

Deirdre laughed throatily. "I know Colter will be sorry he wasn't here. With his callous sense of humour, he would have found our meeting very amusing."

"Would he?" Natalie challenged coolly, fighting for the self-respect that Colter seemed intent on denying her, directly or indirectly.

The question was ignored as Deirdre smiled sweetly, silent laughter in the green eyes at Natalie's bristling stance.

"I realize that slaving around the house the way you do, there must be a thousand things that need to be done, so I won't keep you, Mrs. Langston."

"Slaving" had been a poor choice. Involuntarily Natalie jerked her head when it was used. She had the fleeting impression of a cat cleaning its whiskers in satisfaction as Deirdre started towards the front door.

"Give Colter," deliberately the redhead hesitated as she glanced over her shoulder at Natalie with a knowing smile, "my love, will you? I'll see him another time."

Natalie was rooted to the floor, frozen by her anger, an anger divided in equal shares among Colter, Deirdre and herself. When the door clicked shut, it took her a full second to realise that Travis McCrea had walked in as Deirdre walked out. Velvet brown eyes searched her rigidly held expression of unconcern behind which Natalie's anger smouldered.

"Are you all right, Natalie?" Travis asked quietly.

"Of course." But there was a brittle edge to her airy reply.

The immediate grim line that tightened his mouth made Natalie realise that she had betrayed herself. She quickly averted her face and walked over to needlessly plump a cushion on the couch. Natalie had never been one to give way to hysteria, but she was possessed by a frightening urge to throw herself on to the couch and sob out her humiliation.

"Was there something you needed, Travis?" She tried to ask brightly, but it was forced and it showed.

He remained in the open hallway, watching her through the carved walnut poles. "No,"

Travis responded. "I noticed Deirdre's car in the drive."

Natalie met his warm brown gaze, her own swinging over the strong, broad face, the thick brows and the silver wings in his jet black hair. Not for the first time in the last two weeks, she silently wished that if she had been determined to make a loveless marriage for Ricky's benefit, she could have married this strong, quiet man instead of Colter. But hindsight never changed anything.

Shrugging self-consciously, she said, "Deirdre stopped over to offer her congratulations."

"I'll bet," Travis mocked drily. "What she really wanted was to meet the woman who snared Colter when she'd failed."

"Snared? That's a joke," Natalie laughed bitterly. "I'm the one who's trapped." Immediately after the slip was made, she regretted it. She sank dejectedly in the nearest chair, wearily pressing a hand to her suddenly throbbing temples. "I'm sorry, I shouldn't have said that. It's not true."

"You can't pretend in front of everyone, Natalie." Although he was still standing in the hallway, his voice seemed to reach out to touch her in reassurance. "Taking my meals at the house as regularly as I do, I haven't needed much insight to see that you and Colter don't act like newlyweds.''

"Please." Her head moved in a negative shake. "The way I feel right now, if you say another kind word, I'll break into tears." As quickly as she slumped into the chair, she pushed herself out of it, determinedly squaring her shoulders. "I have what I wanted and I'm not going to start complaining simply because my loaf of soft bread has a hard crust."

Travis nodded an understanding, a glint of admiration in his eyes. His head turned slightly towards the door just as it opened and Colter walked in. His blue-green gaze swung from Travis to Natalie and back to his foreman with aloof detachment.

"Is something wrong?" Colter inquired, pulling off his leather gloves and tossing them on the small table.

"No, I was just leaving," Travis replied, and set his wide-brimmed hat on his dark head. "I'll see you tonight, Natalie," he offered in goodbye as he opened the door.

When the door closed seconds later, Colter stared at it in a thoughtful silence that scraped at Natalie's raw nerves. She stiffened instinctively as his gaze flicked derisively to her.

"Travis doesn't usually come to the house during the day," she stated defensively.

"Neither do I," he reminded her. "But today I want to shower and change before I drive into San Antonio."

He turned from her and started down the hallway to their bedroom, his fingers making short work of the buttons on his shirt. Anger raged within Natalie that he should casually ignore her. She was in no mood to be brushed aside so easily, and she followed him down the hall.

"Are you going with Deirdre?" Natalie asked with deliberate softness, as she stopped just inside the door of their bedroom.

Colter laughed softly. "I wondered how long it would take before you got around to her."

"She was here earlier."

"I know." He unbuttoned the cuffs of his shirt and sat on the bed to remove his boots. "I was just leaving Flo's cottage when Deirdre stopped by to see her. Was that why Travis was here? To rescue you from her clutches?" he mocked, rising to his feet and stripping the shirt from his back. The marks left by her fingernails were clearly visible on his naked shoulders. "Perhaps he doesn't know you can defend yourself."

"He's more of a gentleman than you are," Natalie retorted.

Colter's ever alert gaze studied her with amused indifference from his handsome but otherwise impassive face. He tossed his shirt to her.

"Throw that in the dirty clothes basket," he ordered.

Fuming silently, Natalie wadded the shirt in her hands, toying with the idea of throwing it back at him, only to dismiss it. In the end, she would pick it up and put it in the hamper anyway. He was watching her face, seeing the silent argument flitting across her features, and his mouth quirked in satisfaction as she walked to the hamper.

At his mockery, Natalie threw caution to the wind, hurling the shirt back to land at his feet. "Throw your own dirty clothes away!" she flared. "I'm not your maid!"

"Deirdre said you might be upset," Colter said lazily.

Fury carried Natalie across the room, halting her a couple of feet in front of him. Before the rubbery sensation that was attacking her legs could take hold in the rest of her, she struck out at him. The paralysing sting of her palm felt oddly pleasant as she glared her dislike. The lean hard cheek bore the pale imprint of her hand that he hadn't attempted to stop, the colour slowly changing to red while his eyes glittered with cold blue fires.

"I don't want that woman in my house!" Natalie raged.

"Your house?" The searing softness of his voice was like a rapier thrust through velvet.

"Yes, my house," she repeated, her wrath too fully aroused to notice Colter's. "I legally sleep with you, which makes it as much my house as yours—if not more, since I take care of it. And I don't want that woman to set foot in it again!"

"If she so desires, Deirdre will continue to come here whenever she likes," Colter stated. His mouth thinned into a forbidding line.

"No! I don't care how many mistresses you have, but I will not tolerate the humiliation of having them paraded beneath my nose!" she insisted vigorously.

"The only things you tolerate are my money and my home." His sarcasm lashed out at her.

"And your touch," Natalie jeered.

Colter's lip curled derisively. "What makes you pretend that you don't like my caresses?" he demanded contemptuously. "Is there some virtuous part of you that denies physical desire exists?"

"You egotistical beast! What makes you think you're so irresistible?" She tilted her head back to look full into his face with haughty disdain.

Blue diamond chips raked her length with suggestive thoroughness and Natalie's blood started to race like fire through her veins.

"Shall I show you?" he asked with a growling purr.

The blazing topaz flames in her eyes sputtered and died, her bravado rapidly fading. Her senses churned with quivering awareness, traitors to her pride. The cutting edge of his diamond gaze slashed away the attempt of her lips to form a protest.

Mutely Natalie spun away. A retreat, however cowardly, was more strategic than the unconditional surrender Colter had planned. But her move was anticipated as his fingers closed over the soft flesh of her arm and pulled her back. With her free hand, she tried to push herself away from his naked chest, a futile attempt that failed when he applied pressure to the small of her back, moulding her to his muscular thighs.

There was no mercy in his slow, torturing embrace. His strength was superior. Even when she gained the use of her other hand after he had released her arm, Natalie could not ward him off.

Arched away from him, her face twisted to the side to elude his kiss, she felt the scorching touch of his mouth against the slender curve of her throat. Unhurried, Colter explored the pulsing vein of her neck, the hollow of her throat, and, pushing aside the collar of her blouse, sought out the sensitive areas of her shoulder.

The unending assault retracted its leisurely trail to her neck where Colter nibbled sensuously at her earlobe, sending waves of unwilling ecstasy shuddering through her body. That insidious, primitive desire was growing inside her. It was only a matter of time until he claimed her lips and she would be lost.

"Damn you!" Her whispering curse sounded more like a sob. "Let me go!"

His mouth moved along her cheek and she felt it curve into a smile as Colter rubbed his jaw against her smooth skin.

"Not yet." The seductive pitch of his voice was riddled with mocking laughter.

Her fingers closed over his jaw and chin and tried to push away the mouth that was roaming at will over her eyes, cheeks and forehead.

"Please, stop," Natalie gasped, unwillingly begging for her release, her pride cast aside to be regained, she hoped, when she was free of his touch. "Deirdre can come any time," she promised. The corner of her mouth was being teased by his warm lips. "You can start a harem in the house. I don't care! But let me go!"

"Would you have me ignore my wife for a harem?" Colter mocked huskily.

"You have to go to San Antonio," she protested as his mouth slowly began moving over hers. His hand was cupped under her chin, preventing her from moving away.

"Kiss me," he commanded against her mouth.

He was being deliberately provocative, tantalising her lips with the nearness of his without kissing her. There was a building hunger to know the elemental mastery she had experienced before.

"No," Natalie refused, fighting with every stubborn fibre of the resistance she possessed.

The arm around her back tightened with crushing force. "Kiss me," Colter repeated with ominous softness, "or we'll still be here when Missy and Ricky come home."

A helpless moan escaped her trembling lips. Instantly the tense muscles around her mouth relaxed. Instinct and experience gained from Colter guided the tentative movement of her lips against his. At first he remained passive under her touch, letting Natalie find out for herself the fine art of initiative rather than response as she began an intimate and mobile exploration of his lips, growing bolder until she felt the answering warmth of his.

Not another action was directed by conscious thought. For Natalie it was like almost drowning, then bursting to the surface and feeling more alive than ever in her life. His bruising ardour was matched by the urgency of her lips. Shock wave after shock wave quaked with primitive tremors through her body.

When Colter gradually eased his mouth from its possessive claim of hers, Natalie was incapable of the slightest movement. Shaking hands rested on his naked shoulders while her head remained tilted back. Behind her closed lashes, she could feel his gaze inspecting the passion still written on her lips.

"Tell me again," Colter jeered softly, totally in control, not reeling from the physical impact of their embrace as Natalie was, "that you only 'tolerate' my touch."

Tears of hurt anger shimmered in her eyes, stinging and smarting like salt on a wound. "I did what you ordered," Natalie said in a choked, trembling voice. "Now will you let me go?"

The expressive lift of his shoulders mocked the stubborn hold on her pride in the instant before he released her completely. Yet the distance between them didn't erase the memory of his hard body pressed against hers, nor the exciting fire that had consumed her. She couldn't meet his eyes that glittered now with a greenish hue. She walked slowly to the hallway door, pausing in its frame.

Without turning around, Natalie said, "I hate you, Colter. Or is hate another emotion that you don't recognise?"

His only reply to that question was an abrupt laugh. "I shall be home for dinner tonight, my loving wife," he mocked sardonically. "So, please, no poisonous mushrooms or arsenic, or I shall be forced to make you eat it so you can die with me."

"And I was planning to spend the rest of the afternoon looking for some deliciously deadly mushrooms," Natalie quipped sarcastically, and hurried into the hall, knowing her barbs were ineffectual but needing them just the same.

The next week Natalie threw herself into a frenzy of activity, inventing cleaning where it wasn't needed, outdoing herself in the cooking of their meals, taking part in excursions with Missy and Ricky, working until all hours of the night to avoid the bedroom. She was never entirely certain that Colter was asleep when she did slip between the covers. He never said a word, viewing her devotion to the house and children with derisive amusement.

Her weight loss was becoming apparent again and the weary circles of exhaustion were faintly making their presence known. Natalie had not thought the telltale signs were visible to anyone but herself.

As she glanced into the oval mirror in the dining room, she pinched her cheeks in an old-fashioned effort to bring colour to her face before entering the living room to let Colter and Travis know that dinner was ready. As had become her habit of late, Natalie addressed her announcement to Travis, her tired spirits brightening a little under the warm glow of his regard.

"Ricky and Missy are at the table, so dinner is ready whenever you are," she said.

"How about giving me five minutes to finish this beer?" Travis asked, holding up his half-empty frosty glass of beer. "I've been dreaming about a tall, cold one all day and I hate to rush it down."

"It was warm today," Natalie agreed, not looking directly at Colter but supremely conscious of his sinewy length stretched out in the chair.

"Warm?" A black brow was raised by Travis at her understatement. "It was practically a furnace out at the pens," he corrected quietly. "A case of cold beer would have been as refreshing as a blue norther sweeping in from the Plains for the hands out there today. I hate to think about tomorrow."

Natalie remembered how gritty Colter had looked an hour ago when he came in from the spring round-up. His shirt had been stained with perspiration and dirt. The bleached brown of his hair had been a dusty shade even with the shield of his wide-brimmed hat. At the time he had looked hot and tired, not the vitally fresh and masculine man that was visible in her side vision now.

"Why don't you ask Natalie to bring out a case of beer tomorrow afternoon, Travis?" Colter suggested lazily, studying the film of foam coating his empty glass when she glanced at him in surprise.

Travis gave him a long look before draining his glass. "Natalie has plenty to do without running out to the pens."

"Oh, she won't mind." The hard line of his mouth turned upward at the ends in a mirthless smile as Colter directed a darkly sardonic glance at Natalie. "My wife," he said with sarcastic emphasis, "enjoys filling every waking hour of the day with an endless assortment of tasks."

Her gaze fell away under his abrasive thrust, catching for a split second the questioning and concerned glance that Travis gave her. The blood mounted briefly in her face, Colter's subtle jibe finding its mark.

Fixing a bright smile on her mouth, she turned to Travis. "Of course, I'll bring out some beer tomorrow. It won't be any trouble. Now, if you will excuse me, I'll go and dish up the soup."

"We'll be right there," Travis answered.

No other mention was made of the way Natalie was working. During the meal Travis kept the conversation centred on the children and their activities. After they were finished, Travis stayed only for coffee, then left. Natalie had no idea where Colter disappeared to after the table was cleared. She didn't think she had heard the car leave, but she wasn't going to check.

With the same determination that had got her through the week, she spent the biggest share of the evening with the children. At eleven o'clock she was still in the kitchen, cleaning the overhead hanging lamp. The night air was still and uncomfortably warm.

Standing on the table top, Natalie wiped the perspiration from her brow with the back of her hand. The downward movement of her head brought a figure into focus standing in the doorway. She turned with a jerk, nearly upsetting the soapy pan of water at her feet. Water sloshed over the side as she recognised Colter leaning against the door jamb. She turned quickly back to her work.

"Did you want something?" she asked icily.

"I thought I would show you the way to get to the cattle pens tomorrow," he answered coolly.

"You're going to show me tonight?" Natalie laughed scornfully. "It's dark outside."

"I meant on the map," responded Colter drily.

Reaching up to wipe the chain with which the lamp was suspended from the ceiling, Natalie hoped she concealed the guilty flush at her own ignorance.

"I'll be finished here in a minute," she said, striving for the coolness of a moment ago.

"No hurry," Colter drawled.

She had been taking her time, but under his watchful eye, she hurried to finish the task. The exertion of stretching to cover every inch and the layers of heat that clung to the ceiling brought a sudden wave of suffocation. The first one Natalie fought off, but the second one had her reeling with a strange giddiness. In the next instant, a pair of hands had closed around her waist and were lifting her on to the floor.

"I'm all right," Natalie protested weakly.

Colter let her lean against the table, removing the hands that disturbed her equilibrium as much as the heat. "Of course you are," he mocked harshly.

"I am. It was just the heat," she insisted.

"I don't particularly care." A thin thread of impatience was in his voice. "You can work yourself into an early grave or simply collapse from exhaustion. Either way, I'm not the one who's suffering the consequences. You are. You can stay here and work for another three hours, but I would like to go to bed. So if you don't mind I'll show you the map now."

If Natalie had thought to gain his sympathy, he had cruelly informed her how misguided her attempt had been. His indifference to her as a woman, a human being, was just as cutting. Suddenly she felt hopelessly defeated.

Silently she followed him as he walked from the kitchen to the small study-ranch office that she never entered except to clean. Her mind had a difficult time concentrating on the pencil tip moving over the large map of the ranch. Natalie could only hope that she remembered the way in the morning. It didn't seem too complicated.

"Can you find it?" Colter asked crisply.

"Yes," she answered dully, resolving to return to the study in the morning after Colter had left to examine the map again.

"Never mind," he sighed in disgust. His eyes had narrowed into blue-green slits as he minutely inspected her face. "You're too tired to even know your own name. I'll show you in the morning."

With that, he turned off the desk lamp, threw Natalie a curt goodnight and walked from the room. Dazed by his complete lack of interest, more hurt than she cared to admit that he couldn't even pretend concern and suggest that she go to bed, too, Natalie stared after him in silence.

He had been right. She was the only one who was suffering. And she had Ricky to think about. What had she hoped to prove? That because Colter was treating her like a slave, she was going to work like a slave from sun-up to sundown?

Colter was in bed when she entered the room. He glanced at her uninterestedly and turned on his side. She continued through to the adjoining bathroom, bathed and changed into her nightclothes. Colter didn't stir when she crawled into bed beside him. A tear slipped from her lashes for no reason that Natalie could think of and she drifted into a tired, troubled sleep.

The house was nearly immaculate from her earlier efforts so the next day Natalie made no attempt to find herself work. As he had stated the night before, Colter showed her the route to the cattle pens. It was remarkably easy and she wondered why she hadn't grasped the directions last night.

Ricky was home in the morning and they spent most of it outdoors before the sun had reached its zenith. He had always been content playing by himself. This morning Natalie sat idly on a lounge chair and watched.

Lunch was not the extensive meal she usually prepared, but just as filling for all its simplicity. She had learned her lesson. She was not going to prove anything else to Colter Langston. Although Natalie still wasn't certain what she had set out to prove in the first place.

The ice chest was filled with cold beer already cooled in the refrigerator, packed with ice cubes to maintain the frigid temperature inside the cans. It was a struggle loading it in the back seat of the car, but Natalie got it in and started for the cattle pens.

It was almost mid-afternoon and it was hot. To hurry would kick up dust on the dirt roads that laced the various sections of the ranch together. Natalie was content to keep a leisurely pace.

Again wildflowers dotted the route, pointing up the greenness of the spring grass and the darker green shade of foliage of the oaks and cedars. She recognised wine cups, bluebonnets, Indian blankets, Mexican hats, and white prickle poppies among the others she couldn't identify. The air was fragrant with their perfumes.

Butterflies and moths flitted from blossom to blossom with the bees while birds encouraged their efforts in song. A silver ribbon twisted through the meadow, and as Natalie turned on to the road that would lead her to the pens, she heard the stream chuckling over the rocks in its bed.

The sound died away and the bawl of cattle began to grow increasingly louder, reaching its fever pitch of intensity as Natalie slowed the car to a stop near the dusty haze that hung over the large pens. As she climbed out of the car, the combined heat of man, beast and sun closed over her with a suffocating hand. The stench of sweat, burning hair, animal discharge and some medicinal odour filled her nose with almost sickening results.

There was activity and movement everywhere as Natalie approached the board pens. Dipping, branding and ear-tagging were carried out with steady efficiency by horse and rider or the man on foot. The rope-swinging, leg-slapping and fast riding so often depicted in western movies was not in evidence. Despite the acrid smells and the unceasing din, Natalie watched it all in helpless fascination.

Shielding her eyes from the incredible glare of the sun, she studied the human occupants of the pen. A few of the men noticed her standing on the roadside, but she was soon forgotten in the unending demand of their work. All of them were dressed nearly the same, dark blue Levi's, the colour of their shirts and hats almost indistinguishable now due to the dust that coated everything.

Yet Natalie had no difficulty at all in picking out Colter from the others. Work-stained like all of them, there was an invisible cloak that set him apart. He sat easily in the saddle of a muscular chestnut horse. Natalie knew he was aware of everything going on around him.

Her concentration was centred on Colter. She didn't notice the horse and rider quietly approaching until the buckskin's head blocked her view. Her startled glance was caught by the gentle caress of Travis's eyes before he swung their attention to the pen.

"What do you think of the exciting, action-packed life of a cowboy?" he asked drily. "Heat, stench, noise and ill-tempered cows.

Who do you suppose we can appeal to for better working conditions?''

"I suppose the Man Upstairs," Natalie smiled, tilting her head back to look up to the broad-shouldered man in the saddle, squinting her eyes when her hand could no longer shield them from the sun's glare.

"You should have a hat if you're going to be out in this sun," Travis commented with a vague note of genuine concern.

Natalie thought of her wide-brimmed straw hat with its bright artificial flowers. It was strictly the garden and pool-side kind, a ludicrous sight out here.

"So I've discovered," was her reply. "I'm a true greenhorn," she sighed. "I didn't realise there were so many things involved in a round-up."

Travis smiled broadly. "It's more than rounding them up and branding the calves. They all have to be run through chutes and dipped for disease. The sick and crippled have to be separated and doctored. The calves are branded and ear-tagged with the bull calves being castrated to be sold later as feeding steers. None of it's romantic or fun."

Natalie coughed as a cloud of dust swirled around her, kicked up by a cow trying to elude a snaking rope. "I agree," she said in a voice still choked by the dust. "The beer is in the back of the car. Do you want me to get it?"

Travis's gaze shifted out to the pens in quick assessment. Colter was quietly walking his horse around the small herd in a route that brought him to the fence rail where they were.

"What do you think, Colter?" Travis asked. "Break now or finish the rest of this herd?"

Colter's reply was unhesitating and Natalie guessed the decision had been made before he had ridden over. "We'll finish this group and run the last herd in. They can be settling down while the men are resting."

He hadn't even glanced at her. She couldn't stop the rigid tensing of her jaw. "How long will that be?" she asked.

There was a brief sliding glance over her face before Colter dismissed her from his attention. "Half an hour or more."

"Am I supposed to stay?" Her voice was taut and weary-sounding as Natalie tried to hide her growing resentment at Colter's impersonal attitude. "I still have to fix the roast for dinner, and Missy and Ricky will be coming home soon."

She was pinned by the sharp edge of his steel-blue gaze, his chiselled features dispassionate and aloof. "You can go or stay, whichever you want, but don't come crying to me about how much you have to do. If you want a shoulder to cry on," he glanced with mocking scorn at the tall, rugged man astride the buckskin, "I'm sure Travis would be more than happy to offer his." A dark, angry flush crept into Travis's tanned cheeks, drawing a curling smile on Colter's ruthless mouth. "As a matter of fact, Travis, why don't you ride to the house with Natalie and bring the pick-up back for the ice chest? You'd like that, wouldn't you?"

With a contemptuous light still in his eyes, Colter reined his horse back to the centre of the pens. Self-consciously Natalie looked away from Travis. She had guessed that he liked her, but Colter had deliberately implied that his affection was deeper. What was more humiliating, Colter didn't care.

"That man is too damned observant," Travis muttered savagely beneath his breath. "He notices things that are none of his business."

Natalie studied him through her lashes, although Travis never looked at her as he dismounted and waved to one of the men to take his horse. Angry resentment was in every severely controlled move as he vaulted the fence and walked to the car with Natalie trailing in sympathetic embarrassment behind him. In brooding silence, he took the ice chest from the car and carried it easily to a spot of shade under an oak. A jerky movement of his large hand signalled that she should drive.

When they were back on the road to the ranch house, Natalie glanced hesitantly at the darkly handsome man in the passenger seat, his arm resting on the opened window, a tightly clenched fist pressed to his lips, as he stared unseeingly out of the window.

"Travis, I'm—sorry." Her fingers nervously clutched the wheel. "Colter shouldn't have said that."

"Why? It's true." A muscle in his jaw jerked as he spoke. "I should have handed in my notice that first week you came when I realised the way I felt," he said with calm acceptance.

There was little Natalie could say. She couldn't offer him any encouragement, especially when her feelings towards him were limited to friendship and admiration. Yet the thought of being deprived of his steadying companionship, of facing all those meals alone with Colter's indifference, struck cold chills in her heart.

They both were silent the rest of the way to the ranch. Natalie realised that Travis had not wanted her to speak. For her to say that she was only fond of him would have been just as cruel as giving him false hope. He was not the type of man to read what he wanted into her silence. At the same time, there was a sense of assurance that he would be there if she ever needed him, with no questions asked and no strings attached.

Her mind kept asking if things would have been different if she had met Travis and Colter together at Fiesta San Antonio. The answer should have been easy. But there was the uncomfortable discovery that it was not. Another question loomed to the front. Why would she have chosen Colter over Travis? That answer eluded her as well.

CHAPTER SEVEN

THE START of Ricky's riding lessons had been postponed until after the spring round-up was over. Natalie had decided to wait and refresh her own skills while Ricky learned. On the day of the promised event, Ricky had awakened when the eastern sky was a lemon dawn. It had required nearly all of Natalie's ingenuity and patience to keep him occupied at the house until the appointed hour they were to meet Colter at the barns.

Ricky had persuaded Missy to come and watch and she was now trailing after Natalie while Ricky impatiently blazed the way, hopping from one foot to the other at Natalie's slower pace. Colter was just walking out of the corral gate when they arrived. Ricky darted past Colter through the open gate, intent on the horses tied to the rails inside.

"Which one is mine?" he asked excitedly, never taking his rounded dark eyes from the two horses.

"The bay on the left," Colter answered.

"What's his name?" Ricky breathed. Now that his horse was in view the need to hurry seemed to have fled.

Colter shrugged. "Joe."

"Joe?" Dislike for the name was evident in the boy's tone and his wrinkled nose. "That's not a good name. I'll call him Lightning," Ricky decided.

Natalie had studied the two horses in silence. The stocky bay that Colter had identified as Ricky's was the same size as the sorrel standing beside it, perhaps even more muscular. She had anticipated that Ricky's mount would be a pony if not a small horse.

A frown of concern creased her forehead as she glanced to Colter's impassive face. "Ricky's too small to ride a full-grown horse."

"A small pony can be just as hard to control as a big horse," Colter replied firmly. "There isn't a better horse around than Joe. You could set off a stick of dynamite beside him and he wouldn't bat an ear."

"His name is Lightning," Ricky corrected. "Can I ride him now?"

"Walk over and untie his reins and bring him here," Colter ordered. "Be sure to come up on his side so he can see you."

Ricky was off like a shot. Involuntarily Natalie stepped forward, her mouth opening to add her own words of caution to Colter's clipped commands. Steel fingers closed over her wrist.

"Let him be." A thread of steel also ran through Colter's quietly-spoken words. "You can't do everything for him."

"He's so small," Natalie gulped. Her gaze skittered away from the blue-green shimmer of his eyes and the tawny gold of his hair. She wished for the steadying influence of Travis instead of Colter's unsettling presence.

"If you're going to become hysterical, go back to the house," was his callous response.

Pressing her lips tightly together, Natalie resolved not to voice any more of her inner apprehensions and suffer Colter's ridicule. She watched in controlled silence as Ricky was swung into the tiny saddle on the horse's broad back.

All of Colter's instructions during the first lesson were crisply worded in a no-nonsense tone. Several times Natalie wanted to explain what Colter said in simpler terms that Ricky could understand, but held her silence, discovering minutes later that Ricky seemed to understand the adult level of Colter's orders. Not until the lesson was over, one that was much too brief as far as Ricky was concerned, did Colter indicate that Natalie should try her horse.

After she had awkwardly circled the corral the first few times, most of her forgotten skill returned. But under Colter's critically appraising eye, Natalie felt less than adequate. Only once did she feel a glow of satisfaction, and it wasn't due to her efforts.

Missy, who had been painfully silent all the while she had sat on the top rail of the corral, watching first Ricky then Natalie, had finally made a comment. "Natalie should keep her heels down, Daddy," she said.

Natalie had seen the swift glance Colter had given his daughter, but he had merely called out to Natalie to confirm Missy's observation. Two thoughts had occurred to Natalie simultaneously. The first was that Missy wasn't quite as reluctant to ride as she said and the second that Colter wasn't as indifferent to his daughter as he seemed.

When the lessons were over and the horses were cooled off, unsaddled and turned out to graze, the four of them walked back to the house. While Ricky was bragging to Missy about his prowess in the saddle, Natalie tried to thank Colter for giving the lessons, which she knew were the first of many. Somehow, in her wording, she managed to convey the wrong impression and received a cynical look from Colter.

"Are you trying to say that you appreciate my time but you would prefer Travis?" he mocked.

Her eyes widened. "No," she protested quickly. "I only meant that I appreciated you keeping your word with Ricky and teaching him to ride."

"Did you think I wouldn't?" Again his blue gaze slashed at her.

"No, I did think you would—" Natalie began defensively.

"But you thought I would have someone else teach you, is that it?" Colter interrupted with a humourless smile.

"If you're trying to say that I was looking forward to spending time alone with Travis, then you're quite mistaken." Her voice trembled as indignant anger took hold.

"I didn't say that at all. You did," he responded complacently.

"But you were thinking it," she retorted.

In a series of fluid movements, Colter halted her steps with a hand on her wrist, turned her to face him, and cupped her face in the firm grip of his fingers. There was a mercurial rise of her pulse as she stared into the enigmatic depths of his green-turquoise eyes. Their attention was centred on her parted lips.

"Do you know what I'm thinking now?" he asked with deceptive softness.

Her legs were suddenly rubbery and her hands touched his waist for support. A jolting current was transmitted to Natalie, almost rocking her back on her heels.

"The children," she whispered in protest at the slow descent of his head.

His hand had moved from her arm to the soft pliant flesh of her back, obedient to his every command. She felt the warm breath of his silent laughter an instant before his mouth closed over hers. She shuddered once in resistance before yielding to the exquisite pressure of his kiss.

Almost before it had begun, Colter moved away. Natalie swayed slightly towards him. His hand slid lightly from her throat to her shoulder, stopping her. This totally physical reaction she had to his touch drew a sigh of dismay from her throat. Would this betrayal of her pride never stop? she demanded silently. She loathed him. Her lashes fluttered upwards, but she saw he wasn't looking at her.

"What is it, Ricky?" Colter asked calmly.

With panic-stricken swiftness, Natalie turned her head to the small boy standing in front of them, Colter's hands still holding her prisoner. A thoughtful frown creased Ricky's forehead as he stared at Colter.

"Do you like all that kissing stuff?" he asked, screwing his face up in dislike.

"It's like spinach," Colter answered in an amused tone. "You begin to like it when you get older."

"Oh," Ricky nodded, the subject no longer of interest to him. "Come on, Nonnie. You said we could have some cookies and milk."

"I'm coming," Natalie murmured, slipping free of Colter's unprotesting hold.

Keeping her eyes downcast, she followed Ricky to the house, vividly aware of Colter's catlike footsteps behind her.

Her and Ricky's riding lessons continued for a week, held in the cool hours of the morning under Colter's supervision. Ricky's sturdy, tractable bay was anything but Lightning, although he obeyed the slightest command—right or wrong—that the reins in Ricky's small hand gave. The commands were more often wrong than right. The uncanny way the horse sensed each time Ricky lost his balance and slowed to a walk or a stop to allow him to regain his seat endeared it to Natalie's heart.

Her own efforts were much more successful. And she found that under Colter's tutelage, she learned more about riding a horse than just staying in the saddle. There was a glow of accomplishment on her face when she circled the corral at a walk, a trot, and a canter, executed a series of figure eights and received not one criticism from Colter.

"We'll go out after lunch," he said as Natalie dismounted, "and see how you do in the open country."

She darted him a look of suppressed excitement, wanting to express her joy and knowing he would regard it with mocking amusement. So she simply nodded a silent agreement and walked away to cool her sorrel, keeping the sensation of triumph locked inside.

After the lunch dishes were cleared and Ricky was safely on the school bus for his afternoon session, it was a different story. Natalie paused on her way to the barns to stand beneath an oak tree and gaze at the verdant meadow stretching out below her. Her mind's eye pictured the image of herself cantering the sorrel over the meadow, a slight breeze blowing her hair. It was an idyllic image that soon was to come true.

She hurried her steps along the path through the trees, breaking into the sunshine a hundred feet from the corral. There she stopped short, the colour draining from her face. Her sorrel was hitched to the outside rail of the corral with Colter's blaze-faced chestnut beside it. Colter was tightening the saddle cinch.

But it was the flashy black and white pinto impatiently stamping the ground and tossing its arched neck only a couple of feet away from Colter that Natalie was staring at, her happiness departing with the speed of a supersonic plane.

Astride the spirited pinto was Deirdre Collins, sophisticated and chic in her split riding skirt of rust brown with a matching vest over a white blouse. A flat-crowned, wide-brimmed hat of the same shade of brown accented the fiery lights of her long hair caught at the back of her neck. There was smug satisfaction in the emerald green eyes as she studied Natalie's look of stunned dismay.

"There you are, Natalie," Deirdre called out gaily, directing Colter's unreadable glance in her direction. "Colter and I have been waiting for you."

Natalie unconsciously bristled at the familiar way Deirdre coupled her name with Colter's. Her chin lifted with rigid pride as she forced her feet to carry her to the pair.

"I didn't know you were here, Miss Collins, or I would have been here sooner," she replied curtly.

That remark drew a melodious laugh from the redhead which angered Natalie further. She cast an accusing glance at Colter's lazily watchful eye. The mocking light in his blue-green eyes subtly reminded her of her rash statement after

Deirdre's last visit to the ranch, the time she had tried to elude his embrace by promising that Deirdre could come any time. And Natalie flushed in silent outrage.

"Daddy was checking some cattle not too far from here," Deirdre was saying. "I decided at the last minute to go with him and ride over for a visit. When Colter told me he was taking you for your first cross-country trip on horseback, I invited myself along. I hope you don't mind."

"Of course not," Natalie replied stiffly.

"I can't imagine what it's like learning to ride," Deirdre added in a patronising tone. Her gaze shifted from Natalie to Colter, an intimate expression in their green depths. "Colter and I were practically born in the saddle."

A chill vibrated Natalie's nerve ends. Her riding ability was no match for theirs. She could feel her confidence already dissolving. Her stomach churned sickeningly as she saw herself forgetting everything that Colter had taught her. There was a terrifying urge to flee before she was humiliated by their superior skill and became the object of silent ridicule.

Colter untied their horses, walking to Natalie and passing her the reins of the sorrel. His perceptive gaze swept her face with mocking thoroughness. His whipcord length blocked

Deirdre's view of Natalie's trembling hands as she took the reins, but he had noticed them.

"You forgot your hat," he said drily.

"My hat?" Natalie echoed blankly. "I don't wear a hat."

"There hasn't been any need for one in the mornings, but you certainly can't ride in this midday sun without one," Colter stated firmly.

The reins were clutched tightly in her hands while the humiliating image of herself in that wretched sunhat with its ludicrous flowers flashed through her mind. Mutinously she averted her head.

"I don't need one," she answered tautly, placing a hand on the saddle horn to mount.

But Colter's fingers dug into the sleeve of her blouse. "I said go to the house and get your hat."

Poisonous gold flecks sprang into her eyes as she met his unrelenting gaze. Then her gaze flickered past him to Deirdre, who was watching their silent battle of wills with obvious pleasure. Without a word, Natalie wrenched her arm free of his hold and angrily tossed the reins at him. Then she spun around and stalked towards the house, resentment blazing in every rigid muscle.

How long would they wait for her to return? she wondered with trembling rage. Because she had no intention of riding with them, certainly not with that stupid hat on top of her head. With impotent fury, she slammed the front door behind her and didn't slow her strides until she reached the kitchen. She stood by the table, needing a release for the rage that consumed her.

Yanking a bucket and brush from a closet, Natalie shoved the bucket beneath the taps in the sink, poured a generous amount of ammonia in the bottom and filled it with hot water. Seconds later she was on her hands and knees on the floor, stripping the wax from the surface with savage scrubbing motions of the brush. The floor was half-done when she heard the front door open and the commanding summons by Colter for her. Her mouth tightened grimly, but she didn't answer.

Nor did Natalie glance up when his footsteps stopped in the doorway of the kitchen. "I thought I told you to get a hat," he said with ominous softness.

"I'm busy," she snapped, dipping the brush in the soapy water and sloshing it over the floor.

"You are going riding." Each word was concisely and emphatically spoken.

"You and Deirdre will find the ride infinitely more satisfying alone, I'm sure," Natalie responded sarcastically.

She rose to her feet, setting the pail of water on the table while she began to move the kitchen chairs out of the way, aware of the steel gaze that followed her every movement and uncaring for its harshness.

"Are we going to go through this again?" Colter demanded. Natalie didn't reply, but mutinously kept moving the chairs. "Are you going to get your hat or am I?"

"Go and get it if you want," Natalie shrugged indifferently, "but I am not going riding."

"Because of Deirdre?" he jeered harshly.

In a fit of temper, she stamped her foot on the floor, turning to face him in a trembling rage. "I am not going to have that woman making fun of me! I don't care what you do to me, but I am not going to wear that ridiculous hat!"

There was a slight tilting of his head to the side in curious amusement. "Ridiculous?" Colter repeated.

"Yes, ridiculous!" she flashed. "You know very well that the only hat I own is that straw one with the flowers!"

Laughter rumbled from his throat, taunting in its mockery.

"It is not funny!" Natalie declared in a voice that quivered with uncontrollable anger.

But the low sound continued. Before she took the time to consider her actions, Natalie was reaching for the bucket of soapy water and emptying it in his direction. Only a few scattering drops fell on him as he side-stepped the bulk of it with ease. Silence splintered the room. Then the glint of reprisal was focused on Natalie through narrowed eyes.

Intimidated in spite of her own anger, she took a hasty step backwards as Colter moved forward. She forced herself to stand still, fighting the cowardly inclination to run while her heart pounded in her throat. She succeeded until he towered in front of her. Too late Natalie tried to pivot away.

Her shoulders were seized in a punishing grip and her back was pulled roughly against his chest. The outline of his masculine form was impressed on to hers. Quicksilver shivers raced up her spine as Colter buried his mouth on the taut curve of her neck. His hands glided smoothly down her arms, sliding on to her stomach, their erotic touch igniting the kindled desires of her flesh.

"You made me do it, Colter. You shouldn't have laughed." The words vibrated huskily from the emotion-charged tenseness of her throat.

Under the drugging influence of his touch, she hadn't the will to resist when he turned her into his arms. His warm bruising mouth moved sensuously over her lips as he easily lifted her off her feet and cradled her in his arms.

"Fire should be fought with fire," Colter murmured mysteriously, his head moving a tantalising inch from hers.

Her arms had instinctively circled his neck for support. As he burned her mouth with a fiery kiss, his statement wasn't nearly as mysterious as it had seemed a moment ago. Natalie was distantly aware of the smooth strides he was taking. There was even a fleeting sensation of satisfaction at the thought of Deirdre walking into the house and the livid greenness of her eyes if the redhead saw the way Colter was kissing her.

A blithe, melodious song seemed to fill her hearing like the trill of a bird, and Natalie closed her eyes tighter to savour the joyful sound. His ardent touch was truly embracing her with a buoyant feeling that she was floating on a cloud. Unwillingly she moaned softly when he took his lips away from hers. Blinking her eyes weakly, she could look at nothing but the provocative curve of his mouth.

"So you wanted to get me wet, did you?" Colter mocked softly.

There was a split second of dazed shock at his taunt before she felt him lifting her away from his chest, then she was falling. Her mouth opened to call out and water closed around her, drowning her efforts as she gulped in the chlorinated water of the swimming pool.

The lethargy his kiss had induced was immediately gone, her arms flailing the water to fight for the surface. Coughing and spluttering, she reached the concrete edge, pulling herself on to the deck, feeling like a half-drowned cat.

Pushing the straggling, wet locks of hair from her eyes, Natalie turned to glare angrily at Colter. A wide smile split his usually impassive face, the white flash of his teeth laughing at her predicament. Yet Natalie was mesmerised by the smile, the genuine grin. She had never seen Colter smile and its effect was dazzling.

"I'll convey your apologies to Deirdre," he chuckled.

Not until he had disappeared around the side of the house did Natalie move, suddenly shivering from the clinging wetness of her clothes.

Colter didn't return to the house again that afternoon. But he unexpectedly appeared in the kitchen as she was adding the dressing to the spinach salad she had made for the evening meal. He unceremoniously dumped the boxes in his arms on to the table. Nervously Natalie turned, self-consciously wiping her hands on her apron.

"You have no more excuses for not riding," Colter stated, his impersonal gaze sweeping her face and hair.

There was a rush of pleasure as she recognised a hat box. But she forced herself not to hurry as she opened it and removed an ivory felt stetson hat with a wide brim. The other box contained denim slacks with a matching jacket. She raised her gaze from the clothes to sincerely offer her thanks, wondering silently if his gifts had been motivated by a thoughtfulness for her feelings or by simple practicality.

But Colter spoke before she had a chance. "By the way," he said smoothly, "we're going to have a house guest this weekend. I thought I'd better tell you now so you'd have plenty of time to get the spare room ready."

"One guest?" Ice froze the blood in her veins, almost stopping the beat of her heart. Her temper would never allow her to endure Deirdre's company for an entire weekend.

"Yes, only one." Colter studied the betraying quiver of her chin. "Why?"

"No reason," Natalie shrugged, carefully folding the clothes back into their box. She closed her eyes tightly at the pain in her chest and shoved the slacks on top of the jacket. Her fingers curled tenaciously over the edge of the table. "Did you have to invite her here, Colter?" she demanded suddenly in desperate protest.

"Her?" A light brown brow rose arrogantly. "I never said the guest was a female."

"Oh, stop playing games!" she sighed angrily. "I know you invited Deirdre to pay me back for this afternoon. It's that sadistically cruel streak in you that wants to be certain I'm sufficiently humiliated to remember my place."

"When have I ever been cruel to you?" His metallic gaze locked with hers.

There was a slight shifting of his stance so that she was cornered by the table and a chair, her escape blocked by his lean form.

"With your coldness, your indifference, the aloof, cynical way you mock life," Natalie answered in a quiet but firm voice. "A newborn baby needs more than food and warmth. He has to have affection and attention or he simply dies. Adults aren't any different." She searched his carved mask. "Colter, don't you truly care about anyone? Isn't there someone's happiness that is important to you?"

"Are you trying to save my soul, Natalie?" There was a wry twist to his mouth.

"I guess I'm trying to find out if you have one—if there's anything you would sacrifice for the benefit of someone else," she answered softly, an unexplainable aching throb in her throat.

A surge of restlessness visibly rippled over him. "No." The slicing edge of his clipped answer made Natalie wince. Long, lithe strides carried him to the door where he paused to study her with deliberately arrogant detachment. "Nor do I have any desire to punish or humiliate you," Colter stated. "Our guest this weekend is Cord Harris. A man."

But Natalie found little comfort in his announcement.

On Friday afternoon, the drone of a small plane sounded above the house. Colter had made no further mention of their weekend guest, not even explaining whether he was a friend or a business acquaintance. Natalie glanced through the window, seeing the red plane descending towards the ranch before she lost sight of it in the trees. Was this Cord Harris? she wondered. Colter had not said how he was arriving, although she knew there was a dirt airstrip beyond the barns.

In case it was their guest, Natalie set two beer glasses in the freezer section of the refrigerator to frost. Twenty minutes later she heard the front door open and the sound of Colter's voice and that of another man. Smoothing the skirt of her yellow-flowered dress, she walked through the dining room into the living room.

Hesitating near the middle of the room, she studied the stranger while waiting apprehensively for the two men to notice her. Taller than Colter, the man had raven-dark hair and nearly black-brown eyes. High cheekbones emphasised the patrician look of his features. The suggestion of arrogance was there, too, not so blatantly forceful as Colter's because the stranger's was tempered by a ready smile.

"Where's Flo?" the man asked in a richly resonant voice. "I expected her to meet us at the door."

At that instant the man's dark gaze swung to the living room, but Natalie had already braced herself for the startled, curious look that sprang into his eyes. The very fact that he had expected Colter's aunt indicated he was unaware of Natalie's existence.

"Hello." There was a faint quiver of anger in her voice, her smile taut with the discovery that Colter had not mentioned her.

"Didn't I tell you when you called that Flo had retired?" Colter asked with infuriating calmness. "More or less, anyway. With her church and charity work, she's hardly ever at home."

"No, you didn't tell me." A narrowed look of hard appraisal was turned on Colter by their guest.

"Then I probably forgot to mention my wife," Colter went on, impervious to the suggestion of censure as he directed the tall, dark-haired man's attention to her. "This is my wife, Natalie. Cord Harris," he introduced with an off-hand gesture.

A rueful smile accompanied the hand Cord Harris extended to her. "I feel I must apologise for my ignorance," he murmured.

"Don't, please," Natalie refused, her chin lifting in proud defiance. "It was a very quiet and quickly arranged ceremony."

Colter's level gaze was locked on to her face. "What she means is that we met at the Fiesta and slipped across the border to get married."

His detached explanation left no room for any romantic construction to be placed on their hasty wedding. That goaded Natalie into discarding any pretence that their marriage was based on love.

Amber lights were still flashing in her eyes as she swung her gaze to the man at Colter's side. "You see, Mr. Harris, I met all his requirements. I could cook, keep house, and liked children." Before either of them had a chance to respond, she rushed on. "Would you two like a beer?"

"Yes," Colter said drily. "That's a good idea."

With the slight inclination of Cord's head in agreement, Natalie walked swiftly from the room, her hold on her temper almost snapping completely. In the dining room, she was halted by the accusing demand she heard Cord Harris issue to Colter.

"What kind of marriage is this, Colter?"

"It suits us," was the shrugging reply. "At least I'm not twisted around a woman's finger the way you are."

"Some day you're going to get brought to your knees," Cord stated grimly, "and you're going to find that it's a position that's not so much humbling as it's enlightening."

Silently Natalie wished those words were prophetic and not wishful thinking. She would like to see Colter grovelling for a woman's affection. She brought them their frosty glasses of cold beer and would have retreated to the kitchen had not Missy and Ricky arrived home from school at that particular moment. After a shyly affectionate greeting, Missy dutifully introduced Ricky, who was as usual not the least bit bashful in front of the stranger.

"Didn't Aunt Stacy and Josh come with you?" Missy asked.

"Not this time," Cord answered with the patient attention of a man who genuinely likes children. He glanced at Natalie to explain. "Stacy is my wife. She and our little boy usually come with me any time I'm on a horse-buying trip. But our own annual registered quarter horse sale is only a couple of weeks away. Colter was best man at our wedding. I know Stacy will regret missing this opportunity to meet you."

"I would like to meet her, too," acknowledged Natalie.

There was a funny ache in her heart at the way he so caressingly spoke his wife's name and the special light that appeared in his dark eyes whenever he mentioned her.

"How old is your little boy?" Ricky piped up.

"Nearly three," Cord answered.

"He's too young to ride a horse," Ricky told him sadly.

"A bit." A barely suppressed smile edged the corners of Cord's mouth. "Although sometimes he rides with his mother or me."

"I've learned how to ride by myself," Ricky announced importantly. Then he darted a cautious glance at Colter. "Almost," he qualified.

"That's enough visiting for now," Natalie said quietly, knowing Ricky would continue without pause if he had a willing participant. "Go change out of your school clothes. And don't forget to change your shoes."

"I'll make sure he does, Natalie," Missy offered tentatively.

Natalie smiled her thanks.

"Missy doesn't seem quite as reticent as she did before," Cord Harris observed after the two children had left the room.

Colter's glance slid thoughtfully to the taller man. "She's become attached to the boy. She's very fond of him."

Cord fixed his attention on the light reflecting through the amber liquid in his glass. "That's understandable. She had a lot of love to give and no one who seemed to need it."

"We've known each other a long time, Cord." There seemed to be a hidden warning in Colter's statement and the two men exchanged measured looks.

Natalie felt the sudden tension, the clang of hard steel when two forces of equal strength meet. It was almost with relief that she heard the front door open and Travis walked through. There was a veiled look to his brown eyes when he glanced at her, but they still managed to convey a silent greeting before he turned to the other men.

"Karl looked at the plane's engine and carburetor, Mr. Harris," he said. "He couldn't find anything wrong, but he suggested that you should call in an airplane mechanic to be safe."

"Is something wrong with the plane?" Natalie frowned.

"It cut out on me twice on the way here, but I didn't have any trouble after the first hour of flight," Cord explained. "The annual inspection on it was just a week ago. I'm sure it's all right," he smiled thoughtfully at Travis. "Thank Karl for checking it out, will you?"

"I will," Travis nodded, and left.

With Travis's departure the two men began discussing the merits of the brood mares Cord Harris had come to see with the thought of purchasing one or more of them. That brief friction that had occurred only minutes before was ignored or deliberately forgotten.

CHAPTER EIGHT

"Can I have a ride in your airplane, Mr. Harris?" Ricky requested.

"Ricky!"

Natalie's sharp reproval failed to silence him as he glanced up, a serious frown drawing his brows together as he met her quelling look.

"But I've never been in a plane yet," he reasoned.

"Not this time, I can't take you up," Cord Harris apologised. "Maybe the next time I come I'll have more time, but now I have to go home. My little boy is waiting for me." He turned to Natalie and offered his hand. "Thank you for having me here."

"There's no need for thanks. You're welcome any time," she insisted.

The dark-haired man bent to Missy, brushing her cheek with a light kiss. "I'll bring Josh when I come again," he promised with a wink, and she smiled in return.

Then Colter was walking with him to the plane, a red Cessna parked on the edge of the airstrip. Over the weekend, Natalie had observed the unusual regard Colter held for Cord Harris. Of course, Cord Harris was a man whom nearly everyone would respect and admire whether they hated him or liked him. The unusual part was that Colter did.

A small sigh quivered from her throat as Colter rejoined her and Ricky and Missy. She studied him surreptitiously from the corner of her eye. This man standing beside her, her husband, a bronzed sun-god, she wondered if she would ever understand him. She knew him intimately and didn't know him at all.

Natalie wondered if she would ever solve the enigma of her own ambivalent emotions towards him. On the one hand, she despised him for the way he used her. On the other she kept being drawn to a fiery inner core that she seemed to catch glimpses of without ever being certain it was there.

The scarlet and white plane taxied to the near end of the dirt runway. The rudders and ailerons were checked. Brakes were set and the motor revved. Then the flaps were partially lowered. Cord saluted them in a final goodbye as he gently rolled the plane on to the strip, quickly gaining momentum.

As Natalie watched the wheels lifting from the surface as the plane became airborne, she

wondered if Cord Harris understood her husband—if he could explain the coldness that
permanently encased Colter. In Natalie's rare
visits to Flo Donaldsen's cottage, not even Colter's aunt had been able to say why he had been
deprived of the capacity to care.

Lost in the labyrinth of her thoughts, Natalie
had been watching the plane without seeing it,
deaf to the sputtering sound coming from its
engine. Ricky's fingers tugged her arm.

"What's wrong with the plane, Nonnie?" he
asked.

By then the engine had died completely and
the red plane was sliding quickly towards the
ground, past the end of the runway and with
insufficient altitude to glide safely back to the
clearing. A few scattered trees stood in its path.

The white El Dorado in which they had all
ridden to the grassfield was suddenly in her vision. She glanced in startled surprise to her side
only to discover that Colter was no longer
standing next to her. While she had been paralysed by what was happening, he had been reacting.

"Missy!" Natalie grabbed the young girl by
the shoulder, the thin face as white and frightened as her own. "Run to the barns and get
help! As fast as you can!"

Without a word Missy turned and ran with Ricky following. Now Natalie ran, not in the direction of the barns where the children were going, but towards the beckoning white rear of the car and the disappearing airplane. The crunching crash of metal on to ground and trees came next, seeming to go on forever yet lasting only fleeting seconds.

As she raced by the end of the runway through the trees, the sound of a pick-up truck came from behind her. Catching her breath against a tree-trunk, Natalie glanced over her shoulder, wanting to wait for the help that was arriving and knowing every precious second might count. Resolutely she pushed herself away from the tree and stumbled on.

As she arrived at the crash site, her stomach turned sickeningly at the sight of the twisted wreckage of the red and white plane. Terror filled her heart, and she felt sure no one could survive that mess of tangled steel. Then a movement claimed her attention. It was Colter straining to open the caved-in door. Sobs tore at her throat at his supreme effort that was doomed to futility.

The pick-up truck squealed to a halt behind her. With rounded, pain-filled eyes, Natalie looked over her shoulder at the men vaulting from the truck, focusing her gaze on the broad form of Travis McCrea. The shattering of glass sounded from the wreckage and she turned to see Colter tearing the broken fragments from the windshield of the plane.

Then her vision was blurred. At first, she thought, from tears. Her lungs expanded slowly in building fear as she recognised the cause of the shimmering haze. In confirmation, there came the crackling of flames. The air was expelled from her lungs in a heart-ripping scream.

"Colter!" This time Natalie screamed a name, her heart filled with terror that he would die along with Cord. "Colter! No!"

Now the fire was visible, hungry flames eating their way from the snarled tail section towards the wings and the ruptured fuel tanks. In that freezing second of utter danger, Natalie knew she didn't want Colter to die as she had so often thought. She loved him! She wanted him to live!

With a smothered cry, she started running towards the plane. Fear impeded the co-ordination of her movements. Grey-white smoke was beginning to change into grey-black smoke, hiding him from her sight. Then her shoulders were caught in a fierce grip. She struggled uselessly against it, sobbing Colter's name with every breath she drew.

"You'll get yourself. killed!" Travis's voice implored angrily.

"I don't care!" Natalie cried. "I've got to reach him. Colter—" Tears gushed from her eyes as Travis failed to listen to her pleas.

Then she heard his whispered, "My God!"

Twisting her head around, Natalie saw a figure emerging from the smoke. With a sharp stab of relief, she recognised Colter's lanky form and the bulk of Cord Harris's tall, heavy body in his arms. Then the flames reached the fuel tanks. The force of the explosion knocked Natalie off her feet, catapulting her to the ground with Travis's protective weight shielding her from the bits of debris.

Flames and black smoke billowed into the air. Suffocating, searing heat tore at her lungs before she was pulled to her feet by Travis and pushed away from the inferno. The green leaves of the surrounding trees were transformed into curled ashes floating aimlessly through the air, suspended by the torrid currents from the fire.

The impetus of Travis's hand pushed her several feet away. But Natalie had no thought to save herself. Turning back, she wanted only to reach Colter. The other ranch hands were of the same mind as she saw them racing to his prone figure, spreadeagled over Cord Harris in an instinctive effort to protect him from the exploding flames.

Two of the men pulled Colter to his feet. Semi-conscious and dazed, he was led and half-carried a safe distance from the burning wreck. The other men, Travis amongst them, were making a human stretcher of their arms and carried the inert body of Cord Harris to safety.

The screaming wail of sirens was in the distance as Natalie's quivering legs carried her to Colter's side. There was the crimson of blood staining his chest, arms, and hands. His hair had been singed by the flames.

"Colter, are you all right? Are you hurt?" Tiny sobs shook her voice.

"Don't worry about me." Despite the growling force of his words, there was a glazed look to his eyes as he pushed her away. She had obstructed his view of the two men bending over Cord Harris. "We've got to get him to the hospital."

"The ambulance and rural fire trucks are here now." Travis was beside them, a restraining arm across Colter's chest. "But I'm afraid it's too late."

The words wiped the glazed look from Colter's face. With a lightning movement, he pushed Travis's arm away, swinging his hand up in a vicious backhand slap that staggered Travis.

"No!" Colter shouted. Cold fury twisted his handsome features. "Damn it! He's not dead! He was alive when I pulled him from that plane!"

"Oh, Colter, don't," Natalie sobbed, trying to stop him as he made his way towards the limp form on the ground.

The only hands he respected were those of the white-coated ambulance attendants arriving on the scene. The look in those green-blue eyes terrified Natalie as he stared at the blood-marked face on the ground. It was as if he was willing Cord back from the dead.

"He must be bleeding badly inside," Natalie heard one of the attendants mutter.

"I feel a pulse," the other one whispered as though he was afraid he would frighten it away. "Weak, but it's there."

With practised skill, the body was slipped on to the stretcher and carried to the ambulance. Colter followed, linked by some invisible wire to the unconscious but living Cord Harris. As the doors swung shut, Natalie turned to Travis.

"Get Flo to watch the children," she ordered.

Without giving him time to acknowledge, she raced for the white El Dorado, sliding behind the wheel and reversing the car almost before the motor had turned over a second time. The ambulance siren screamed for her to follow and she did, its wavering shriek so like the ebb and flow of life.

At the hospital, the admitting nurse directed Natalie to the surgical wing. There she found Colter sitting on a couch in a small alcove off the corridor. He was leaning forward, elbows on his knees, his hands clasped in front of him, staring at the closed doors marked "Surgery." His gaze flicked to her in impersonal identification as she sat down beside him. Except for the hand she placed on his thigh, she made no gesture, uttered no words of reassurance. At the moment, all of them seemed without meaning.

The minutes dragged with immeasurable slowness and they waited in mindless silence. Colter was like a statue carved from stone, tensely rigid and unmoving except for his eyes that followed every person who left or entered the surgery doors.

With no conception of how much time had passed, Natalie saw his gaze narrow as a short, ageing man stepped through the surgery doors. He was not gowned in the familiar green of surgery. A white coat flapped about his legs as he walked purposefully towards them, his face permanently drawn in lines of gruffness.

"I thought I told you to get those hands taken care of," he snapped at Colter.

"They're only scratched," Colter growled.

"Scratched?" the man scoffed. "Filled with dirt and glass, too. There's nothing you can do here except pray. He'll either be in there for hours while they try to put all the pieces back together or it'll be over in minutes."

"Cord is going to live," Colter stated, his eyes vividly blue in challenge.

"Are you asking me or telling me?" the man mocked. "Because if you're asking me, the only one who can answer that question is God Almighty. All that can be humanly done is being done. The authorities have notified his family."

"His wife—" Natalie began.

"She's flying in, although I don't know how she has the guts after what happened to her husband." The man reached down, taking a firm grip of Colter's arm. "Come on. We'll get those hands and arms cleaned up."

There was an instant of stiff resistance. Then Colter rolled to his feet, an impatient cougarlike spring to his steps as he followed the man down the corridor. Natalie went along. Her tawny hazel eyes closed tightly at the sight of the slashes on his hands and arms from the broken windshield of the plane. The depth of her love for Colter made her feel the pain he seemed impervious to.

Then his blood-stained and torn shirt was put back on, covering the majority of the bandages except those on his hands. Their silent watch was resumed outside the surgery doors. A nurse brought them coffee which Natalie sipped sporadically and Colter ignored.

More time inched by. Light hurried footsteps sounded in the hall, accompanied by long, masculine strides. Colter was on his feet as Travis appeared with an attractive brunette at his side. She walked straight to Colter, her hands reaching out for his while she mutely smiled a tremulous greeting.

"Are you all right?" Travis asked Natalie quietly.

"Yes," she whispered tautly.

"Dr. Matthews called and suggested I meet Cord's wife at the airport," he explained.

Her gaze turned to the slim brunette, and she was barely aware of the comforting hand Travis placed on the back of her waist. She marvelled at the control in Stacy Harris's voice when she spoke.

"Travis told me the way you risked your life to save Cord." The brunette's words of thanks were softly spoken but without the tremor that blocked Natalie's speech. "There aren't any words to thank you, Colter."

"Cord's thanks will be enough." A muscle twitched in Colter's jaw.

Stacy Harris glanced over her shoulder as if following Colter's gaze to the surgery doors. "He's still in there, isn't he?" A shudder trembled through her and she hugged her arms about her as if to ward off the cold.

"They said it would be some time yet before he's out," Natalie offered in a weak voice.

It was more than two hours before a tall, heavy-set man emerged from the surgery doors, weary and grim, a mask hanging about the neck of his green gown. In a tired voice, the surgeon told them that Cord had survived the surgery, implying that he considered it a miracle. His injuries were extensive and serious, ranging from a severe concussion and broken bones to internal injuries.

"When may I see him?" Stacy Harris asked quietly.

"They'll be taking him from the recovery room later to intensive care. It'll be some time yet," the doctor replied. "He's fighting every inch of the way, Mrs. Harris, and that's about all I can tell you."

"Thank you." A solitary tear slipped from Stacy's curling lashes, the first one Natalie had seen.

A quaking sigh of relief came from Natalie. Travis's gaze flew down to her face in concern and understanding. When the doctor left, he took the edgy silence with him. Colter walked to the window looking out to the west and stared at the sky shot with crimson arrows. Natalie couldn't stop herself from following.

Without glancing at her, he asked, "Is Flo watching the children?"

"Yes."

"He's going to make it," Colter stated.

"Yes," Natalie agreed.

"I'm sending Travis back to the ranch." His gaze flicked from the window to her face. "I know you want to go with him, but you're staying here with Stacy."

Natalie's head jerked away as if he had physically struck her. "I planned to stay anyway," she said through the tight lump of pain in her throat. It felt like her heart. "You are in no condition to drive home with those hands."

He glanced at the bandages as though he had forgotten them entirely. Offering no acknowledgement, Colter turned away and walked back to the small alcove where Stacy waited. He had always had the power to hurt her. Now, with the new-found love Natalie felt, he had even more.

At midnight, Stacy was allowed to see Cord. She returned to the waiting area pale and shaken, but still in remarkable control of her poise. His condition hadn't worsened nor had it improved.

The doctor who had cleaned and bandaged Colter's arms came bustling down the hospital corridor at two in the morning. At the sight of him, Colter stiffened, his head thrown back and a taut line to his mouth.

"What happened, Matthews?" Colter demanded.

"Are you still here, Langston?" the doctor snapped.

"What happened?" he repeated.

"Your friend isn't the only patient in this hospital. You're going to be next if you don't go home and get some rest." The man's scowling face was turned to Natalie. "Take your husband home. The next few days are going to be rough going. He might as well get some sleep while he has a chance. I've already made arrangements for Mrs. Harris to sleep here at the hospital. The nurses will see that she's as well cared for as her husband."

"I don't need any sleep," Colter denied in an expressionless tone.

"Get out of this hospital or I'll have you thrown out." But the doctor's threat made little impression on Colter. A heavy sigh broke from the older man's lips and his expression grew serious. "I'll notify you personally if there's the slightest change either way, Colter, but go home."

"Please, Colter," Stacy added softly. "You and Natalie have done so much already. If the doctor doesn't phone you, I will."

Natalie would have added her own pleas to theirs except she knew Colter wouldn't listen to hers. For once, Colter obeyed someone else's orders. Within a few minutes, she and he were in the car and bound for the ranch. Not one word was spoken between them until Natalie halted the car in the driveway.

"Would you like me to help you wash?" she asked.

"I can manage," he rejected her offer curtly.

When they entered the house, Flo appeared in the living room wearing a long jersey robe to cover her nightgown. Colter didn't even glance at his aunt, but strode purposefully down the hall to their bedroom. It was left to Natalie to bring Flo Donaldsen up to date.

"Travis told me it was a miracle Cord was still alive at all," the woman murmured with a weary shake of her head when Natalie had told her all she knew.

A wave of nausea swept over Natalie as she remembered the terror that had gripped her. "I still don't know how Colter got him out of that plane before it exploded.''

The grey-haired woman was staring sightlessly beyond Natalie. ''I once accused Colter of not possessing any emotion. I was so wrong. So very wrong.''

The amber flecks in Natalie's eyes glowed with sudden brilliance. Colter's reactions had been totally emotional, not just by rescuing Cord, but afterwards when he refused to consider him dead and later again at the hospital. He was capable of very deep-seated emotions. That cold hard shell was only an outer covering that had not been pierced until today. There was a tumultuous leap of her heart.

''You must be tired,'' Flo Donaldsen announced. ''The children are sleeping soundly in their beds and it's time that you did the same.''

''Yes, I am tired,'' Natalie said, but she actually felt marvellously awake.

''I'll take care of breakfast in the morning for the children,'' the woman offered.

''Please wake us if there are any telephone calls from the hospital,'' Natalie asked as she started down the hall after Colter.

''I will,'' Flo smiled. ''No matter what the news is.''

The bedroom light was on. She found his bloody, torn shirt in the bathroom and the evidence that Colter had washed. But he wasn't there. Natalie tiptoed into Missy's room and then Ricky's room, thinking he might have been prompted to check on them. He was in neither. Surely he wouldn't have gone back to the hospital, she thought wildly.

Hurrying through the other rooms in the house, she saw from the living room window that the car was still parked in the driveway. A light was on in his study. When Natalie re-entered the living room, she felt a breeze of night air blow on her face. The french door to the back patio stood open.

Stepping into the darkness, Natalie saw Colter almost instantly. He was sitting in one of the chairs, his legs stretched out in front of him, his head tilted back to stare blankly at the sickle moon. She started to speak, then she noticed the can of beer in his bandaged hand, the metal catching the faint glow of the moonlight. As she watched, his fingers moved, slowly tightening around the can, unconsciously crushing the aluminium container without his even noticing the liquid that spilled down his hand.

"You're supposed to drink the beer," she murmured softly, walking over to remove the can from his hand, "not spill it all over the patio."

Colter sighed, but didn't reply, although she felt his gaze move to her face.

"It's going on four o'clock," Natalie smiled at him gently, loving him so very much that it was almost a physical pain. "Won't you come to bed?"

In a slow, reluctant motion, he rose to his feet, but made no move to enter the house. She wanted desperately to tell him that she understood the silent anguish he was going through. Fear held her words in check, fear that he would reject her sympathy. She stood uncertainly at his side, wondering if she should repeat her question or simply leave him.

"Colter." She said his name with an aching throb in her voice. "You need to rest."

"Do I?" His voice, husky and warm, vibrated around her, physically touching her with his evocative tone.

"Yes, you do," she whispered.

With a fluid turn, Colter faced her, his features hidden in the shadows, the moon trailing a silvery pale light over his light brown hair.

"How long has it been since I've touched you, wildcat?" Behind the soft caress of his words was the harshness of mockery that she knew so well. Her watery knees threatened to buckle.

"Please, Colter," casting aside the surging need his question had aroused, "I want you to rest."

A soft chuckle came from the shadows of his face. "But that's not what I want." Hard decision laced his statement.

Her breath was drawn in sharply as his hands closed over her hips and she was pulled against his male hardness. Before she could control the sudden explosion of her senses, his mouth was covering hers with searing hunger. Her lips parted on contact, allowing him to take all the sustenance he desired. His appetite was ravenous as he demanded the full satisfaction of the melting softness of her body.

Then Colter broke free and an inaudible sigh broke from Natalie's lips to feel again the consuming fire of his kiss. Steel fingers closed over her wrist, biting into her flesh. Ignoring her involuntary cry of pain, he pulled her through the patio doors, the glass rattling in the panes as he slammed them shut. The momentum of her shaking legs carried her to his side. Using it, Colter swept her into his arms, the gauze of his bandages scraping the bare skin of her arm. For an instant it broke the seductive spell of his touch.

"Colter, your arms," Natalie protested faintly. "You're hurt!"

There was no reply until they reached the bedroom, where he let her feet swing to the floor. His arm still circled her waist, moulding her against his length while his other hand brushed the hair from her cheek.

"Then don't fight me tonight, Natalie," he murmured.

The beat of her heart fluctuated wildly as the bedroom light illuminated his expression an instant before it was switched off. The forbidding set of his jaw was there and the unrelenting line of his mouth, but there was no remote indifference in his eyes. They had blazed with desire— for her!

CHAPTER NINE

SUNLIGHT DANCED over her face, warming her skin with its golden kiss. Natalie snuggled deeper into the embrace of the strong arms that held her.

"I was beginning to think you were going to sleep until noon," a low voice whispered into her hair.

Keeping her eyes tightly closed, Natalie smiled dreamily and slowly moved the top of her head against Colter's chin. The scent of his maleness was like a heady wine. She was afraid to speak, afraid to let all the sensations of love come spilling out.

"You're a bewildering creature, Natalie," Colter murmured, shifting her into a more comfortable position and bringing her nearer to his face on the pillow.

"Why?"

The smile remained when her lips moved to ask the throaty question. Her lashes fluttered partially open to let her eyes drink their fill of his handsome face. There was a jade glitter to the eyes that were roaming lazily over her features.

With his usual arrogance, he ignored her question. "I'm hungry. Get up and fix me some breakfast." The order was softly given, closer to being a request than a command.

Reluctantly Natalie untangled herself from his arms, instantly missing the warmth of his bare flesh against hers. In the darkness of last night, it had been easy to conceal her love from him. The brilliant sunlight would undoubtedly reveal the love she wasn't ready to acknowledge.

There was a desire to keep it to herself a little while longer. Colter was much too observant for her to hide it from him forever. Besides, she wanted him to know. But she wanted to tell him in a moment that was not heavy with the aftereffects of passion.

Her gold robe was lying on the foot of the bed and Natalie reached for it as she slipped from beneath the covers. Quickly stepping into it, she zipped it to the top, then glanced at Colter. He had pushed himself into a half-sitting position with the pillows at his back. The white of his bandages stood out starkly against the tan of his face and chest. The half-closed look with which he gazed at her exhibited a lazy thoughtfulness.

"Bacon and eggs?" Natalie questioned, and he nodded. She started towards the door. "It shouldn't take long. Would you like me to bring it on a tray?"

"I'm not an invalid," he said drily, "but if I'm not there when it's ready, I guess you could bring it here."

The hands of the kitchen clock indicated that it was nearly midmorning. Missy was in school and from the window over the sink, Natalie could see Flo Donaldsen sitting in one of the patio chairs. She guessed accurately that Ricky was playing somewhere nearby.

As she began placing the bacon strips in the square skillet, the door in the kitchen leading outside opened. With a happy smile, Natalie turned to greet Flo, but it was Travis who walked in. He stopped at the sight of her, the expression on his ruggedly handsome face freezing a little.

"Good morning, Travis." Some of the happiness that bubbled from the eternal fountain of her love crept in to add an airy lilt to her voice.

His mouth moved into a smile that didn't reach his eyes as her greeting gave him back his mobility. "Good morning, Natalie. I was just bringing in the mail," he explained, tossing envelopes and magazines on the table.

"Is there anything important I should take to Colter?"

"Not that I noticed," Travis answered slowly. "Is that his breakfast you're cooking?"

"Yes, he's still in bed," Natalie answered.

There was a husky undertone in her voice, placed there by the vivid memories of the ardent lovemaking they had exchanged in the pre-dawn hours.

"You look especially radiant this morning." His dry observation veiled the sparkle in her eyes. The hand holding the fork paused above the bacon-filled skillet as Travis asked, "Is there a reason?"

"Yes," she answered, suddenly conscious of his feelings towards her.

His hands were resting on his hips in a vaguely challenging stance. "The look of a woman in love, perhaps?"

She bent her head for an instant, wishing she didn't have to hurt him although she had never once thought that she might be in love with him. Then she slowly turned to him, giving him a faint look of apology but not regret.

"Surely you guessed earlier the way I felt," Natalie prompted gently. Travis had been there at the crash site when she had discovered she loved Colter.

Dark lashes shut out the look of pain in his brown eyes, a momentary look that was gone when Travis opened his eyes. "I guess I couldn't believe that it happened."

"It did happen," Natalie smiled faintly, "and I wouldn't change the way I feel for all the money in the world."

His long legs moved him towards her in slow deliberation, his brown gaze searching every corner of her face. "I want you to be happy, Natalie," he said with taut control. "May I— kiss the happy bride?"

She hesitated for only a second before she turned her face up to his. With both hands, Travis framed her face as if memorising each feature. Tears shimmered in her amber eyes at his pain. He lowered his head towards her lips.

"For all the times I'll never hold you, Natalie," he said in a husky, aching whisper.

Then he was kissing her, the pressure of severely checked passion trembling the mouth that claimed hers. But his possession was short, drawing away from her as he breathed in deeply. The twisting pain of lost love marred his rugged face in the instant before he spun away towards the door. Natalie wanted to call out to him, to say something that would ease his hurt. She was the cause of his anguish, so there were no comforting words she could offer.

Robbed of a little of her joy, or more correctly sobered by the discovery of the harsh side of love, Natalie turned back to the breakfast she was preparing for Colter. Minutes later, she was sliding the eggs on to a warmed plate and adding the bacon. Juice, coffee and toast were already on the tray where she set the plate. Humming lightly to herself, Natalie picked up the tray and started for the door. It burst open before she reached it and Ricky came tumbling in.

"Morning, Nonnie," he cried gaily.

"Good morning, Ricky. Good morning, Flo," she added brightly to the older woman, who had followed Ricky at a more sedate pace.

"Are you just eating breakfast?" Ricky exclaimed in a scolding tone. "I'm going to help Flo get my lunch."

"I'll take this to Colter and come back to help you," Natalie winked.

"Colter isn't here," Flo frowned her surprise at Natalie's words. "Ricky and I just talked to him in the driveway. He's on his way to the hospital."

"But he asked me to get breakfast." She stared in blank confusion at the older woman.

"All I know," Flo shrugged in sympathy, "is that he said he'd telephoned the hospital. He didn't sound satisfied with the information he received. I imagine he forgot all about eating.''

"He could have told me he was leaving," Natalie said in a protesting murmur.

"Colter isn't in the habit of informing anyone about his plans," Flo reminded her.

That was true, Natalie admitted. She had rarely known where he was during the day. Yet surely after last night—she shook that thought away. His thoughtlessness had been caused by his concern for Cord Harris. She could not fault him for that.

Colter didn't return for the evening meal, although Natalie postponed serving it for nearly an hour in hopes he would come. Nor was Travis there, sending word to the house in the afternoon that work would be taking him to the opposite end of the ranch. Flo had naturally returned to her cottage, which left only Missy, Ricky and Natalie sitting around the large dining room table.

It was after midnight when Natalie heard the crunch of the wheels in the gravelled drive. Uncurling her legs from the sofa, she closed the book in her hand, completely aware that she had been reading the same page for over an hour without grasping a word, and tossed it on the adjacent cushion. She opened the front door before Colter's hand could touch the knob.

"Hello." Natalie smiled in accompaniment to her breathless greeting.

"I thought you'd be in bed." His gaze flicked over her tiredly as he walked by.

"I waited for you," she explained unnecessarily. "I wasn't sure if you'd eaten and I wanted to know how Cord was."

"He's still listed as critical, but his condition is improving, so the doctors say," he sighed with bitter scorn. "I'm not hungry. Deirdre and I ate at the hospital cafeteria."

"Deirdre?" Natalie questioned hesitantly. "You mean Stacy."

"No, they sent her a tray so she could stay with Cord."

Unconsciously she followed as he walked down the hallway to their bedroom, briskly removing his jacket as he went. She tried to ignore the sinking in her heart.

"What was Deirdre doing there?" Jealousy goaded her pride into asking the question.

"She heard about the accident. So she came to the hospital to see how he was and if there was anything she could do to help," Colter answered sharply.

"Does she—know Cord and Stacy?"

"No," he mocked sarcastically, "Deirdre always offers her sympathy to complete strangers. Of course she knows them!" he snapped.

As he tugged at the sleeves of his shirt, Natalie saw him wince involuntarily when the material caught at the adhesive of his bandages.

"Let me help you," she offered quickly, stepping forward to ease the material over the gauze.

"Save your mothering for the children." Colter pulled away from her touch, giving her a look of savage irritation. "I don't need it."

Hurt pride lifted her chin to a defiant angle as Natalie turned away, leaving him to struggle on his own. With jerky movements, she began her own preparations for bed, trying to convince herself that Colter was tired and worried. Slipping the nightgown over her head, she heard the bed accepting his weight.

"Flo said she would stay with the children tomorrow," Natalie said stiffly.

"What for?" Colter asked uninterestedly.

Natalie glanced sharply over her shoulder, her gaze sliding away from the impersonal hardness of his. "So I could be with Stacy," she said, averting her face from his remote eyes.

"There isn't any need."

"Why not?" Natalie challenged, the clinging nightgown whirling about her legs as she turned quickly around. "You wanted me to last night."

"That was because you were available."

"And I suppose Deirdre will be at the hospital tomorrow," she murmured cattily.

His gaze narrowed. "Yes, she'll be there and so will I. You're a stranger to Stacy. Deirdre and I have known her since she married Cord. Besides, it's more convenient."

"Why convenient?" Natalie demanded, jealousy tearing at her heart.

"Because Deirdre has an apartment in town. She can be at the hospital in minutes if Stacy needs her."

There was a betraying quiver of her chin as she met his mocking eyes. "Maybe you should stay there," she suggested sarcastically as she walked stiffly towards the bed. "It would be more convenient than driving back and forth."

"I'll consider it," Colter said levelly, and rolled on to his side.

The trembling of her chin started other quivers through her body. Her emotions, muddled and confused, touched off conflicting urges. She wanted to scream at Colter to go to Deirdre now, to throw things at him and arouse him out of his indifference if only to gain his anger. She wanted to bury her head in the pillow and cry with frustration and the futility of her love. Most of all, she wanted to touch him, to apologise, to make him understand that she didn't want to fight him—she wanted to love him.

In the end, Natalie did none of those, but switched off the light and slid beneath the covers to lie in rigid silence listening to his even breathing. Why had she thought anything had changed, she asked herself, simply because for a short time the night before Colter had desired her?

Natalie was awakened the next morning by the sound of closet doors opening and closing. Through the curtain of her lashes, she watched Colter shrug into a shirt of light blue print and tuck it into the waistband of his denim slacks. As if he sensed her eyes on him, his piercing gaze swung to her. Its discerning quality made feigning sleep impossible. Natalie forced her eyes to open slowly, moving her shoulders to pretend that she was just awakening.

"Don't bother to get breakfast for me," Colter drawled, reaching for the matching jacket on the chair.

"Will you be home for dinner tonight?" she asked as though his presence was of supreme indifference to her.

"If I'm not here, eat without me," was his clipped reply.

But the very fact that he had answered in that way forewarned Natalie that he wouldn't be home. The entire day and night she was tortured by fears that her spiteful words had driven him to Deirdre, although she silently realised that no one could make Colter do anything he hadn't already decided to do.

Refusing to humiliate herself by waiting up for him again, she went to bed shortly after Missy and Ricky did, tossing and turning until she fell into a troubled sleep. She didn't hear him return. The only evidence that he had consisted of the clothes he had worn lying on the chair and the rumpled pillow beside her own.

For two days, Natalie didn't see Colter, only signs that he had returned to the ranch. On the afternoon of the third day, she, Ricky and Missy were at the corrals where Ricky was resuming the riding lessons that had been interrupted. This time they were under Travis's supervision, since Ricky had appealed to him the night before.

Ricky was cantering the stocky bay around the enclosure. The horse's front hoof struck an outsized chunk of earth and he lurched forward before regaining his rhythmic stride. The slight stumble was all it took for Ricky to lose his balance and tumble to the ground. Travis reached him almost before the first wail broke from Ricky's lips. Natalie and Missy were only a step behind.

"Oh, Ricky darling, are you hurt?" Natalie reached anxiously for the crying boy as Travis helped him from the ground. His little arms wrapped themselves tightly around her as Ricky buried his face in her neck and continued to sob uncontrollably.

"Put him back on the horse." The snapped command came from behind them.

Natalie's arms tightened protectively around Ricky as she turned to glare at Colter, striding towards them in tight-lipped coldness.

"He's been hurt," she protested, but Colter's hands were pulling the child away in spite of his efforts to cling to Natalie and hers to keep him there.

Ignoring Ricky's suddenly increasing cries, Colter carried him to the patiently standing bay and sat him in the saddle, picking up the loose reins and handing them to Ricky.

"Nonnie!" Ricky wailed, clutching the saddle horn tightly and ignoring the reins Colter was placing in his hands.

Natalie tried to rescue him, but Colter's arm swept her away. "You cruel, horrible beast! Can't you see he's hurt?"

Sharp spears of blue steel turned threateningly to the crying boy. "Are you hurt, Ricky?" Colter demanded, and received a tiny nod that he was. "Where are you hurt?" When Ricky failed to answer, Colter taunted, "You're afraid, aren't you?" Ricky's cries had reduced to gasping sobs as he stared wide-eyed at Colter's accusing face.

"Of course he's frightened," Natalie defended. "That's a long way for a little boy to fall."

"He's going to fall off again if he doesn't take those reins," Colter stated grimly, looping them around the horse's neck within Ricky's reach.

Before Natalie could guess what Colter planned, he slapped the horse on the rump, sending it trotting away. Her heart jumped into her throat. There was a terrified look on Ricky's face as he started to slide from the saddle again. Immediately the docile bay slowed to a shuffling walk and Ricky pulled himself upright in the saddle.

"Now pick up those reins," Colter commanded. Without any directing hands on the reins, the bay stopped. Ricky's hands were frozen on the saddle horn. "Pick them up or I'll hit the horse again."

"Colter, for God's sake!" Travis exclaimed angrily.

Colter ignored the protest as he took a threatening step towards the horse. Ricky immediately took the reins in his hand, still shaking and wide-eyed, but the sobbing had stopped.

"Walk the horse around the corral." The harshness was gone from Colter's voice, but the firmness remained. After a hesitant glance at Natalie, Ricky obeyed. At a walk and a trot, Colter made him circle the corral several times. "Now, canter Joe around the corral once," he ordered.

Natalie's mouth opened in instant, outraged protest, only to close in disbelief when she heard Ricky speak. "His name is Lightning." And it was Lightning he nudged into a canter.

"I did a good job, didn't I?" Ricky smiled from ear to ear as he stopped the horse in front of Colter.

"Yes, you did," he agreed, lifting Ricky out of the saddle onto the ground. Natalie started to step forward, but Colter was already instructing Ricky to cool the bay. Then he turned to Missy. "Do you see how it's done?"

The young girl immediately buried her chin in her chest at his question, her thin face pale and drawn. Without a glance at either Travis or Natalie, Colter walked to his daughter and swung her slender length into his arms. There was mute appeal in the clouded blue gaze Missy directed at her father's impassive expression.

But Colter stepped through the corral gate and to Natalie's sorrel horse tied to an outside post. He set Missy in the saddle, untied the reins and climbed up behind her. His arms protectively circled her as he walked the horse away from the corral in the direction of the open meadow beyond the stand of trees.

It was two hours later that Missy came rushing into the house, her face flushed and excited, her eyes sparkling with pride. Her words ran into each other in her hurry to tell Natalie and Ricky of her accomplishment in conquering her fear of riding.

"Daddy said I wasn't to be ashamed that I was afraid. He said being afraid of horses was like being afraid of the dark and I had to learn there was nothing that would intentionally harm me. He rode with me for a long way just talking and making me relax and remember how much fun I used to have riding. Then he got off and I rode by myself for a while. And Daddy said I was almost as good as I used to be, and with practice, I would get better."

Natalie's smile was mixed with astonishment at the animation on the young girl's face. She couldn't ever remember Missy being so confident or talkative. And she wasn't finished yet.

"We talked about a lot of other things on the way back," Missy continued. "Daddy said I wasn't a little girl any more, that I was becoming a young lady and maybe it was time I stopped wearing my hair in braids. Do you think I should get it cut, Natalie?''

"I can make an appointment with the hair-dresser and we'll see what he suggests, but I think you would look very pretty with short hair," Natalie suggested.

"Oh, do you think so? I told Daddy I was skinny and plain, but he said I was probably one of those girls that would bloom late in my teens and just knock everyone off their feet. Can you imagine that?" Missy breathed. "Shall I change into a dress for dinner? Daddy said I would look good in blue because it matches my eyes."

"I think that would be a good idea."

"Come with me, Ricky," who hadn't been able to get a word in edgewise. "And you can help me brush my hair."

As she watched the two of them dash from the dining room, Natalie decided it was amazing what a man's attention could do for a girl. She had always sensed that Colter could be overwhelmingly charming if he chose to be. In the face of Missy's transformation, it was difficult to keep nurturing her anger over the harshly callous way he had treated Ricky, particularly as it had proved correct.

CHAPTER TEN

COLTER DIDN'T come to the house until it was exactly mealtime, his face a smooth mask that seemed to belie Missy's account of their afternoon ride. He pulled out the chair at the head of the dining room table and sat down.

"Aren't we going to wait for Travis?" Natalie asked.

"He won't be eating here." The answer was clipped out with no explanation.

Natalie could only guess that Travis had made other plans rather than observe her with Colter, knowing the way she felt. She ladled the soup into the bowls.

"How is Cord?"

"He responded lucidly to the doctors today. They don't have any more reservations about his recovery." Again that impersonal tone marked his words.

Apart from Natalie's expression of relief at that news, Colter's statement brought an end to the conversation. Without Travis's participation in the routine of after-dinner coffee and with the children excused from the table, Natalie found the continued silence scraping at her nerves.

"Are you going to the hospital tomorrow?" she inquired stiffly, taking a sip of the coffee that was still too hot to drink.

"No, I'll be needed at the ranch now." One arm was draped over the back of his chair as Colter stared with brooding thoughtfulness at his china cup.

Natalie glanced at him quizzically. There had seemed to be a hidden meaning in his reply. His impassive gaze caught her look and the line of his mouth hardened.

"You might as well know," he said with cold arrogance, "I've fired Travis." He glanced at his wristwatch. "He should be packed and gone by now."

"You fired him?" she repeated incredulously. "But why? What did he do?"

"That's none of your business."

"Surely he'll stop to say goodbye to Missy and Ricky," Natalie persisted, unable to understand Travis's abrupt dismissal.

"Don't you want to say goodbye to him?" Colter mocked harshly.

"O-of course," she stammered. "Travis has—has been very kind to me." The sound of disgust that Colter made roused her anger.

"And a gentleman," she added sharply, "regardless of what you think!"

"He's a man," he jeered softly. "I can't believe that there weren't a few stolen kisses."

Uncontrollably Natalie flushed, remembering the innocent kiss she and Travis had exchanged the morning after the crash. Colter would never regard it as innocent.

"Where is Travis going?" she asked instead, striving for composure. "Did he say what he was going to do?"

"Isn't it strange?" Colter chuckled without humour. "You're more upset by his leaving than he is. When I told him he was through, he seemed relieved. I had the feeling contingency plans had been made between you."

"What do you mean?" Her voice was unsteady, sickened by his implications.

"I hope you aren't thinking of running away with him. I can make life very miserable for you."

Hurt anger trembled violently through her. "More miserable than it is now?" Natalie taunted. "I think that's impossible!"

The muscles along his jaw leaped savagely. "We made an agreement and you're going to keep it!"

"And how are you going to make me do that?" she challenged. "Lock me in every night? Post a guard at the door whenever you're gone? I'm not your slave, Colter Langston! I'm not chained to you!''

Her hands were on the tabletop next to her cup, clenched into impotent fists. With a lightning move, his fingers closed over one of her wrists with punishing fury as he leaned threateningly towards her.

"You will do as I say and like it!" he growled.

Her reaction to his imperious arrogance was instantaneous. Her free hand gripped the coffee cup and threw the scalding liquid into his face. Frightened by the cry of pain, Natalie bounded to her feet and raced to the front door, hearing the crash of china and chairs as the partially blinded Colter began his pursuit.

Through the door and into the moonless night, she ran. Fear for her own safety was replaced by prayer that she had not injured Colter. Yet she couldn't go back and endure any more of his insults. His cruel insistence that her wishes and feelings were of supreme indifference to him wounded her more than the falseness of his accusations.

Madly racing for the concealment of the oak trees, Natalie reached them as the front door slammed behind Colter. The black trees hid her from his sight, but the darkness also worked against her. She stumbled over tree roots, was slapped in the face by low-hanging branches, and only the light from the barns glittering through the leaves kept her going in the same direction. As she burst into the open, she heard Colter crashing through the trees.

Her feet were not directed to any particular destination. Her only aim was to escape, momentarily anyway, Colter's retribution. The yardlight flickered over a large metallic object. As Natalie drew nearer to it, she recognised its shape as a pick-up. Then a dark shape separated itself from the truck, rushing out to meet her. For a screaming second, she thought it was Colter.

"Natalie?" Travis's low voice was mixed with surprise and concern.

With a gasping sob for breath, she threw herself into his arms, clinging to the broad chest with what little energy remained. Holding her close, Travis brushed the tangled hair from her face.

"What's wrong? What has he done to you?" he demanded grimly.

"Nothing. Everything," she whispered wildly. "He told me—"

"Take your hands off my wife, McCrea!" Colter's harsh voice sliced off the rest of Natalie's explanation.

"I don't work for you any more, Colter," was Travis's low reply. "I don't take orders."

As Colter walked closer, Travis set Natalie to the side and stepped in front of her, shielding her with his body.

"To get to her, you're going to have to go through me," Travis said, in that same soft undertone that sent shivers of fear racing down Natalie's spine.

"Don't threaten me, McCrea," Colter warned. "I've whipped bigger and stronger men than you."

"You're going to have to do it again. I've stood by and watched long enough while you walked on Natalie with your muddy boots. I'm not going to keep silent any more."

"Travis, please!" Natalie clutched at his elbow to restrain him, the muscles flexed and ready in his arm.

"Keep silent?" Colter's lips curled into a jeer. "Were you silent when you held her in your arms and kissed her?"

The tall, dark-haired man took a threatening step forward. Natalie eluded the arm that tried to keep her behind him and raced in front of Travis, spreading her fingers on his broad chest to stop him.

"Stop it! Both of you!" she cried in desperate anger. A hasty glance at the forbidding faces of the two men told her that her pleas had fallen on deaf ears.

"If Natalie wouldn't end up hating me," Travis went on, "I'd kill you for that remark."

"Are you trying to deny it?" Colter laughed harshly. "Natalie's already admitted you've kissed her."

"He kissed me, yes! Once!" Natalie admitted shrilly, trying to stop the fight that neither man could win. "But not the way you think!" Beneath her hand, she felt the sudden stillness take hold of Travis.

"Why should it matter to you, Colter, that another man finds your wife desirable?" There was an odd watchfulness about his brown eyes as Travis studied the man challenging him. "It never bothered you when men made a play for your first wife. Not even when they succeeded. Why does it concern you that I want Natalie? Or is it that you're afraid that she wants me?"

"She's staying with me," was the snarling reply. As Colter took a menacing step closer, the light illuminated his face, revealing the murderous thrust of his rapier gaze. "All the plans you've made to run away together might as well be cancelled, because there's no place you can go that I won't find you!"

"What's one woman more or less to you?" Travis taunted.

"Get out of the way, Natalie," Colter ordered in an ominously soft voice.

"No." She refused weakly at first, then gathering strength, "No!" Travis made no attempt to stop her as she raced to Colter, digging her fingers into the iron bands of his arms. "I won't let you fight!"

With a casual, shrugging movement, Colter broke free of her grip. The harsh glitter of his eyes swept her face as he took her by the shoulders, mocking her puny attempt to stop him.

"It won't do you any good to try to protect him," Colter told her coldly.

"You crazy, blind fool!" Travis laughed bitterly. "It's not me she's protecting. It's you!"

A sound of disgust came from Colter as he flicked his gaze from Natalie's pleading eyes to challenge Travis. "You don't expect me to believe that, do you?"

"You've finally joined the rest of us mortals, haven't you, Colter?" A heavy sigh broke from the other man's lips as the tension of battle left his muscles. "You've left your mountain lair and now you know what it's like to love someone until it feels like your guts are being torn out."

Natalie gasped sharply at Travis's sardonic declaration, unable to believe there was any truth in it. The hands gripping her shoulders increased their vicelike hold. Her doubting gaze swung to Colter's face. Unearthly pain flickered across the usually impassive and hard features as he stared beyond her at Travis.

"Is it true?" she whispered. Her hands touched his waist, her body swaying closer despite the punishing grip of his fingers. "Oh, Colter, please? Is it true? Do you love me?"

The mask was gone. With aching hunger, his gaze swept her upturned face before he crushed her against his chest, holding her so tightly that she couldn't breathe. His chin and cheek rubbed the top and side of her hair, a rough, feline caress from a mountain cougar.

"Yes," Colter groaned. "Yes, I love you, Natalie."

Quivering sobs of utter happiness shook her frame, tears of joy streamed from her eyes. She hadn't believed it was possible. Drowning in the overflowing cup of her love, she was too choked to speak, savouring the punishing glory of his arms.

In the flicker of an eye, he was shoving her violently aside, striding from her into the shadow of the trees without a backward glance. Stunned by his unexpected action, Natalie could only stare after him for a paralysed moment.

"I never thought anyone could reach him." She pivoted sharply towards Travis's quiet voice, having forgotten he was there. "Without you he'll die, Natalie," he murmured.

There was pain in the brown eyes that looked at her. "And you," she asked softly, compassion forcing her own happiness back for a moment, "what will you do?"

"I'll live," he smiled wryly. "I only looked on you from afar. I won't have those memories of holding you in my arms in the middle of the night."

"You don't have to leave," she whispered.

"Yes, I do. You know that." Travis breathed in deeply, seeming to shrug off the pain. "I've saved some money. I think I'll get a place of my own."

"I wish you all the happiness in the world."

He turned towards the pick-up. "Colter left so he wouldn't stand in the way of what you wanted. He's never before placed anyone's desires above his own. Don't torture him any longer, Natalie."

Her feet began moving backwards. "Goodbye, Travis," she offered huskily before she turned and raced to the house.

But the impetus of her love made it feel more like floating. Flinging open the front door, she paused on the threshold, halted by the stark pain in Colter's eyes as he stood in the hallway.

"I knew you wouldn't leave without Ricky," he muttered, turning his head from her. "May God give me the strength to let you go again."

There was the sound of the pick-up motor grinding to life and the crunch of wheels on the drive before it sped by the house.

"Travis is leaving," Natalie said softly. "I'm not going with him and I'm not going to meet him. I never planned to."

"What do you take me for? Some kind of blind fool?" Colter exploded. A savage fury broke around her as he swung a blazing look to her face. "I came down that morning to have the breakfast I thought you were so lovingly preparing. I heard you tell Travis that you loved him and all the money in the world didn't matter to you! I saw the look in your eyes, all soft and warm, before he kissed you."

"Oh, Colter, no!" She ran to him, her hands touching the muscles of his chest stiff with rage. "I was telling Travis that I loved you! Whatever I said about money was to let him know that I didn't care if you were rich or poor. He asked if he could kiss the bride."

Colter turned away from her in disgust, unable to believe her.

"I swear it's the truth, darling," Natalie vowed in a throbbing voice. "How could I go into another man's arms after what we shared that night? I love only you.'' He stared at her, searching her face, wanting to believe. ''Don't you see?'' she reasoned. ''That's why it hurt so tonight when you kept accusing me of having an affair with Travis. I love you, not Travis.''

''You said life was miserable with me,'' he snapped.

Colter flinched when her fingers touched the muscle leaping so wildly in his jaw. ''Isn't life miserable when you think the one you love doesn't love you?'' Natalie argued softly.

''It's hell!''

As the words were clipped out, he was sweeping her into his arms, burning his brand on to her mouth. She savoured the bruising caress of his hands, needing the reassurance of his love as much as he needed hers. For long moments they strained to break the bonds of physical restriction. Then Colter reluctantly pulled his mouth from hers, gently cupping her face with his hands, breathing raggedly as he rubbed her forehead with his in a surrendering gesture.

''After the way I've treated you, I have no right to your love,'' he muttered in self-disgust. ''At this moment you should be hating me.''

Natalie pressed herself more tightly against his length. ''A thousand times I told myself that I did hate you. There were moments when I wished you were dead. When I saw the plane catch fire and knew you could be killed, I realised I didn't want to live without you. Suddenly I didn't care why you had married me or why you took me to your bed.''

A convulsive shudder trembled through him.

''I never thought I was capable of feeling more than surface emotions. The sight of Cord trapped in that wreckage shattered that illusion,'' Colter sighed, lifting his head to gaze into her face. ''And when you walked into the hospital and sat down beside me, not saying a word, just touching me to let me know you were there if I needed you, I felt—I felt like the lowest creature that ever walked the earth. I understood why Cord had mumbled his wife's name when I pulled him from the wreck. I had this terrible need to have you with me. And there you were.''

''Deirdre?'' she questioned softly.

He looked deep into her glowing topaz eyes. ''I never saw her except when she was at the ranch the times you know about and at the hospital. I had no need to see her. I found too much pleasure in arousing my reluctant wife.''

Gently Natalie kissed his lips. ''I love you.''

There was an exceedingly humble light in his eyes, the proud arrogance gone, the aloof remoteness something belonging to the past.

"There's a lot you're going to teach me," Colter smiled ruefully. "I don't know anything about being a husband or a father. I'd like to get to know my daughter. It's my fault she's so shy and insecure. I now understand the agony of believing that the one you adore doesn't care for you."

"It's simple, darling," Natalie whispered. "All we have to do is draw Missy into the circle of our love."

"And Ricky," Colter added softly, a wondrous smile curving his masculine lips so near to hers, "and all the other children we're going to have."

...And now a tantalizing preview of MOONSPELL by Regan Forest coming soon from...

In September, two worlds will collide in four very special romance titles. Somewhere between first meeting and happy ending, Dreamscape Romance will sweep you to the very edge of reality where everyday reason cannot conquer unlimited imagination—or the power of love. The timeless mysteries of reincarnation, telepathy, psychic visions and earthbound spirits intensify the modern lives and passion of ordinary men and women with an extraordinary alluring force.

If you enjoy this exclusive glimpse at an exciting new kind of romance, look for these titles this September, wherever Harlequins are sold.

EARTHBOUND—Rebecca Flanders
THIS TIME FOREVER—Margaret Chittenden
MOONSPELL—Regan Forest
PRINCE OF DREAMS—Carly Bishop

MOONSPELL
REGAN FOREST

Chapter One

NICHOLAS PAUL was the perfect man. Every woman who met him fell in love with him. Thousands of women all over the world thought of Nicholas when they were with other men, lesser men who could never measure up to Nicholas Paul. He was handsome, rich, talented, exciting. He was larger than life. He was everything.

I was in love with Nicholas, too. I'd lived with him for the past five years, the best five years of my life. I knew him better than anyone in the world and loved him more. He was my Nicky. I created him.

He was born within the memories of my heart, born somewhere inside the folds of my brain—an outgrowth of all the emotions I'd ever known and everything I'd ever learned of men. He came to life between the pages of my books—four books now, four adventures.

Ah, he was wonderful, Nicky was. More wonderful than James Bond who came before him, because he was more human somehow, having been created by a woman. Sometimes the sight of a fallen bird would make Nicky turn his head and stand speechless for a moment or two. Women loved him because he was as tender as he was strong. But Nicky wasn't real. He was my creation.

My name is J. D. Nigel. My friends call me Jaye. For a long time people who read Nicholas Paul books believed I was a man. That's what they were supposed to think, because readers don't trust a woman to write about a world-class insurance detective and sometime spy-adventurer such as Nicholas Paul. No one knew the truth, until recently when word got out that the creator of Nicholas Paul was a woman. But now that he's established, men want to be like him and women want to love him. So I'm getting away with it. Nicky's popularity is growing.

When I travel, though, I don't make an issue of who I am. I travel alone to the places where the adventures are to be set, and there I summon Nicky to bring life to the stories that have been steaming and brewing and growing in my imagination.

Because I have traveled so much, I know a lot of people in cities around the world. I had a good life, an exciting life, until something happened one summer night that abruptly turned my world upside down. That night I lost all certainty of what—or who—was real and what—or who—was not.

IT HAD BEEN a refreshingly cool spring in Spain that year. When I arrived in Madrid in early summer, the mild weather remained and everyone, grateful for each day of cheating the stifling heat that should be descending upon us, was in high spirits. I had brought Nicky here for our latest adventure, one involving two mysterious murders, the first long unsolved, the second, its duplicate in every detail, half a century later.

One of the scenes that I had in my head—the first of those I wanted to write here—was to take place in a café. The cafés of Madrid were not new to me, but as was my habit, I took myself to my setting to make notes of little things overlooked by the eye of my memory.

It's impossible to carry on a conversation in a café in Madrid because of the noise. People don't sit across from one another and talk. They yell. They scream, they pound on the table. Spanish voices are gay and incredibly loud. I was used to that; it was part of the atmosphere. In a corner with my notebook, I reveled in the fun of writing this adventure story and manipulating the famous detective into and out of trouble.

By Madrid standards it was still early; eleven
o'clock and the evening meal was just beginning. I had started to feel hungry myself and
was reaching across the table for the menu when
something drew my attention to the center of the
room. The sight of the man made me draw a
quick breath—a breath that almost hurt. It was
a stab followed by a pain that began in the back
of my throat and traveled down my body to my
chest, my heart.

I stared and kept staring, because there, sitting across from me in the café where I had
conjured up a scene for him, was Nicholas Paul!
The man was exactly Nicholas Paul—the dark
hair, the broad shoulders, the body language,
the way he leaned forward, listening so intently, cocking his head a certain way to hear
what the man across from him was saying. The
way he wrinkled his brow and quirked his
mouth into a small smile that said he could
barely hear, but he was trying. Every gesture,
every look, was so familiar. He was no stranger.

It must have been several seconds before I
noticed what he was wearing, and when I did,
the wild sensations started all over again. My
heart raced and stopped, raced and stopped, as
if it didn't know what to do—any more than my
head knew—because the man sitting there was
wearing exactly what Nicky was wearing in the

scene that I was forming. Dark slacks, a light-weight, white turtleneck summer shirt, fitted tight across the shoulders. I stared at the shirt. How could he possibly be wearing the same thing Nicky was wearing in this café scene in my head?

One part of me—the part that lived in images and daydreams—wanted to get up out of my chair and walk across the room and say, "Hello, Nicky," almost accepting the fact that what I had imagined was taking place before my eyes. But another part of me was frightened. Coincidences like this just didn't happen.

I tried to rationalize. But the fact remained that his face was as familiar to me as my own. I'd seen it in a thousand daydreams. I was in love with that face and that man, real or not.

If I touched him, would he dissolve like vapor? Was he flesh and blood? Or an apparition?

Unable to move, I simply sat and gaped. He wasn't a Spaniard, I decided; his gestures were not those of a Spaniard. Unfortunately, over the din it was impossible to hear what language they were speaking at his table. Blinking, I looked away as one looks away from the blinding sun, but my eyes quickly found their way back to him.

Perhaps he felt my stare, as people do sometimes. He must have, because his eyes flickered
away from the person on whom he'd been so
intently gazing. And his gaze didn't wander
about the room looking for the source of the
energy that was bearing down upon him. Instead he turned his head and looked directly at
me, and me alone.

I was dazzled by his silver-blue eyes, eyes that
flickered with such surprise. His forehead was
knitted in a frown, and every flicker, every
movement of muscle in his face showed surprise. My heart was behaving crazily. I tried to
draw a breath and couldn't, our eyes locked together in a gaze I'll never forget.

He seemed to know me! Yet he couldn't—this
stranger couldn't know me.

Our eyes caught there, above the smoke and
noise of the room. I don't know what he was
seeing, but I was certain of one thing: he rec-
ognized me. He really is Nicky! I thought for
one crazy moment.

Then sanity returned. I began to shake. I tried
to look away and couldn't. He shifted his attention back to the man who was talking to him.
But again his gaze seemed drawn to me.

Stop me from staring! I prayed. Perhaps it
was only my staring that was drawing his atten-

tion; he was simply reacting to that feeling of being watched.

But no, it was more. His eyes were burning me with silver fire. I don't think I even smiled. Neither did he. He just stared at me as if to say, "I almost . . . remember."

Shortly afterward I watched them leave. The man stood taller than the others when he rose. In the shadowy interior of the restaurant his face looked incredibly handsome. Just before he reached the exit, he took a pair of sunglasses from his shirt pocket and put them on. How strange I thought, wearing sunglasses to go out into the night. It made me wonder if he was guarding his identity, hiding from someone—or something.

After he had gone, I sat trying to decide if a dream had indeed walked into—and out of—my life.

NICHOLAS PAUL wasn't exclusively my property—not anymore. The whole world knew him. They didn't know me, but they knew and loved Nicky. He belonged to them, and yet he couldn't come out to play unless I brought him, or have new adventures unless I allowed it. I'd brought Nicky to Spain, and there happened to be a man in Madrid who looked and dressed just like him. A coincidence.

Morning light had a sobering effect, especially in that sunny country where the summer sun rises so brightly over the buildings and splashes like diamonds in the fountains. I tried to get back to work, to forget about this coincidence.

There was a scene forming in my mind, to be set in one of my favorite places in the city—near the magnificent statue of Cervantes. It was a site where Nicky, my hero, would make contact with another undercover detective.

Here I was, creating a make-believe plot while living a true story more diabolical than any I could have conjured up in my imagination....

But I'm getting ahead of myself. Early the next afternoon I sat down under the statue of Cervantes with notebook in hand to soak up atmosphere, record impressions, sounds, smells, feelings in the air on this day at the beginning of summer.

Perched on a stone bench, eyes closed, I could envision the scene clearly. Nicky was wearing dark slacks, a white shirt and a loose, very expensive leather vest, with a pocket on each side. He was waiting impatiently. I heard the voices in Spanish—Nicky spoke several languages, of course—and just as the scene was really coming alive in my head, some invisible force grabbed at me and made me open my eyes. I gasped. There, walking in the crowd was Nicholas!

Again. The same man I'd seen last night in the crowded café. The same man whose eyes had met mine. The same man I'd wanted to rush toward and say "Nicky!"

I scarcely noticed the man with whom he was walking, or anything else . . . except the clothes. White shirt, brown leather vest, expensively cut, with a pocket on each side.

It was too much for me to comprehend. Terrified, I closed my eyes and had to force myself to open them again. I don't know whether I wanted him to be still there, or whether I wanted him gone. The pavement shimmered in the sun, making waves, making everything unreal. The Spanish sun beat hot upon my head and shoulders; its reflection from the chrome of cars was dazzling. I was being blinded and I couldn't see reality anymore. I couldn't really see this man who was squinting in the summer light. My Nicky wasn't real!

Yet he was right in front of me! He'd jumped out of the pages of my book, leaped out of the fountains of my imagination and was sparkling with life, as if he had been given energy from the air and the sun . . . and somehow from me.

I sat gaping. He seemed to feel the visual attack, because without missing a step he looked up, not at the enormous statue above, but directly at me. The way he had last night. A strange thought flashed across my mind: he knew this place well or he couldn't have walked by the magnificent statue, so intent on his conversation that he didn't look at it. Of course. Nicholas Paul had been here many times.

My brain was whirling; I was trying to hold on to the past—before today, before last night. His eyes were on me again, with that same expression of surprise and recognition. He wasn't wearing dark glasses, and the sun seemed to be reflected from his eyes; even at that distance I could see it. No sunglasses in the glare of midday, yet he had worn them last night!

He hesitated. His companion was looking around to see what it was that had caught his attention. I saw that other person only as a shadow; my concentration was on the man who must be Nicholas. For one heart-stopping moment I thought, *he's going to come over here!*

With that same I'm-trying-to-remember wrinkle in his forehead, he halted and almost came toward me, but then stopped himself. After all, he didn't know me.

I shivered and sweat under the weight of his stare. He blinked, perhaps sensing my discomfort. There were people walking between us like slashes of darkness, shadows coming and going, filtering sun between their bodies as they moved. It was hypnotizing. Somehow I knew he didn't have the courage to come near me, just as I didn't have the courage to go to him.

Nor would I have had the courage to touch him. He might have been warm; he might have been cold; he might have been nothing but air. He kept walking, and the moment was gone.

Looking away then, talking to his companion, he was leaving me behind, just as he had done last night. I sat staring after him, at his broad shoulders in the vest and the graceful way he walked. Every movement was so familiar to me. The crowd folded in around him, and like water falling into a fountain he became part of the whole and was gone. Again.

A shadow seemed to move across the sun. Fear was gripping me. Two coincidences? How could there be two? Just the man would have been enough. But the clothes? No, something magical was happening, something other-worldly—something my instincts were simultaneously drawn to and warned away from.

It was all I could do to get myself up off that stone bench and walk, but at the same time I was kicked and prodded by a powerful urge not to lose him. I felt my legs moving under me, moving faster along the sidewalk toward the entrance to the subway where I thought they had gone. I started down the steps, searched the thousand faces, but none was his.

Some hidden part of me, I felt, was gone. Nicholas was a part of me, yet he was eluding me, leaving me. I was so confused!

The memory of that look in his eyes burned in my mind. "You?" his eyes had asked. "You?"

I walked in a daze, feeling the heat of the sun heavy upon my shoulders and thinking, did I make this happen? Did I somehow will him here? Could I have touched him? I walked, not knowing or caring where I was going, and thinking crazy thoughts, wild thoughts, thoughts I could hardly believe were really coming from me.

I'd try an experiment, I decided, to see if I could make him materialize. Not in a public place, where the appearance of any stranger might be construed as a coincidence, but somewhere private. Could I, by planning a scene in my head, make it happen again? I had no choice but to try.

MY MADRID ADDRESS was the penthouse of a friend. It was a sprawling apartment in the heart of the city, so rich in atmosphere that I'd already planned to set some scenes there.

The top floor of the ancient building was reached by a painfully slow elevator from a small lobby off the street. Lydia's flat had three entrances, one a front door, the second an opening onto the rooftop, from where one could look out over the city of Madrid, and then cross to a third door at the far end, which led into the flat's long, narrow kitchen.

Lydia was a secretary for an American-based company in Madrid. We'd met years ago through friends, and she always invited me to stay with her when I was in town. She was a musician when she wasn't at the office, and so were many of her friends. There was an old, unpainted piano in one of the three bedrooms and an even older piano in the living room. Guitars sat against the walls and on the blanket-covered couch, and every corner exuded charm. Sagging, creaking wooden floors, rough, solid old furniture. It was too often cold here in winter and hot in summer, but always welcoming to gypsies like me. Lydia's penthouse was one of my favorite places in the world.

In my book in progress, Nicholas Paul would attend a small gathering here, where he would meet some of the characters with whom he'd share his latest adventure.

That afternoon I set the scene vividly in my mind. How would I dress him for tonight? Still in leather. Nicholas often wore leather. The vest. I could add something, a little flair—something no other man would be likely to wear, for this was an experiment.

A narrow scarf around his throat. Nicky could get away with wearing a scarf, a silk scarf in tones of pale blue and brown and tan. A white shirt, sleeves rolled up. Surely no forces that played with coincidence could come up with a costume like that.

I invited a dozen friends, who could have no way of knowing they were part of a scene. Or of a crazy game. I wouldn't tell any of them that a stranger might be in their midst. The truth was, I didn't really expect him; it would just be too much.

Sherry on the sideboard. Wine, cheese, bread. A gathering to say hello to old friends whom I hadn't yet seen since my return to Madrid two days ago. Arranging the evening, I kept thinking of Nicky as a stranger with the sun—and me—in his eyes, and I walked in a dream.

Lydia was pleased to learn we were having a party. We nibbled the cheese and bread and started drinking wine long before anyone arrived. I said nothing to her about what I was doing. How could I?

It was ridiculous, anyway. A stranger wouldn't show up here uninvited. I *had* invited Nicky in my mind, but how could a living, breathing man walk through that doorway, sprung only from my mind? It couldn't happen. Yet I waited through the longest hours of my life.

The guests didn't begin arriving until nearly ten o'clock, which was typical for Madrid. Trying to calm myself with sherry, I was determined just to enjoy the party, for that was all this was going to be.

It was good to see old friends again and catch up on the gossip. Lydia was at her very best— even a little high, playing her guitar with more skill than she'd exhibited when I'd been here last. It was a hot night. All doors and windows of the apartment were open, letting in the sounds of traffic from the street five stories below, along with muffled shouts and laughter, the barking of dogs.

At midnight some of us were gathered around the piano, singing in English and Spanish; the party was in full sail. I happened to look up and my breath left me, my legs went numb. Nicholas Paul was in the room!

I hadn't seen him enter. I'd forgotten an hour ago to constantly watch the door; the realities of time and the party had served to lessen my be-

lief in miracles. But now he was here, wearing
the vest I'd dressed him in and the scarf around
his neck.

I'm dreaming this, I thought. The scarf
wasn't exactly as I'd envisioned it. The colors
were similar, but it was smaller, and he wore it
tied at the side of his throat. He wore a smile,
too, and that was new. I realized it was the first
time I'd seen him smile.

He wasn't smiling at me; he hadn't seen me.
But people were greeting him, touching him,
shaking his hand, so he couldn't be an apparition. One man, at least, seemed to know who he
was. Someone must have invited him!

Reeling, I swept the cobwebs from my mind,
sorting through the tangle of old memories.
Somewhere there had to be a memory of this
man! Claudio was the guest who knew him.
When had I met Claudio for the first time?
Three years ago when I was here. Nicholas was
five years old; damn, it didn't fit.

When then? When could I have seen him?
When, before the picture of Nicholas Paul
erupted like a volcano in my head? If I'd seen
him, it had to have been five years ago at the
earliest. When could our paths have crossed?

It wasn't here, I knew, because Lydia didn't
know him. And I'd remember. *Surely I'd remember!* My memory was vivid and accurate, a

point of pride. The first time I ever saw the face of Nicholas Paul, it appeared against the blackness of night...appeared clear and strong on the sill of my imagination. I'd seen his face in a vision...not a memory. No, definitely not.

The deeper I plowed through my recollections, the more certain I was that I had never seen this man in the flesh before last night. And even if I had, it still wouldn't make any sense of the distortions of logic that had brought my emotions to a rolling boil. It wouldn't explain how I knew what he would wear or where he would be, even if I'd seen him a thousand times!

My brain-scouring turned up absolutely nothing. I hadn't seen him, hadn't ever known him, and yet we were somehow entangled...frighteningly entangled. Reality had run amok!

Was he really Nicholas Paul—this man who stood across the room...so big, so beautiful and so perfect? No man could be this perfect. I'd known for years that no man could be as perfect as Nicholas. He was created that way. And here I was looking at him, and he was flesh and perfect, and I was speechless and beginning to feel feverish.

He came into the room relaxed, accepting a drink, laughing at someone's joke, while I stood by the piano, taking in his beauty and the miracle of the whole affair, wondering who the hell he was. Wondering at that point who *I* was. I quivered as I anticipated meeting him, I was terrified to meet him...half expecting to be swallowed into my own half-written scene. I'd never been so bedazzled and frustrated and confoundedly confused in my life. Nor ever so awake.

He was lifting his wineglass to take a drink; the glass was in midair, his elbow bent, when his gaze moved up and across the room toward me. His hand stopped moving and hung in midair, as if he'd forgotten what he was going to do; he just stood there, looking at me. And I stared back.

I was strangely aware of myself. What is he seeing? I wondered. My white blouse trimmed in lace, a full, blue cotton skirt, small sandals on my feet, my dark hair pulled back from my face. I might as well have been a mannequin. He was seeing only a mannequin with a stupid and blank expression. I had to move, try to look alive!

He set down his glass without ever taking the intended swallow of the drink. Someone was pulling diligently on his arm, demanding his attention. He turned away reluctantly and was led across the room.

Other people grew fuzzy and time had no measure. Only a few minutes elapsed before he found me. I'd half expected someone to make introductions, but oddly, no one did. I had moved to the kitchen doorway, then turned around and he was there, not smiling, not frowning, just looking at me in that puzzled way.

Approaching, he looked down at me from his great height and said, "Where do I know you from?" Not hello, just, "Where do I know you from?"

THE LOVES OF A CENTURY

Join American Romance in a nostalgic look back at the twentieth century—at the lives and loves of American men and women from the turn-of-the-century to the dawn of the year 2000.

Journey through the decades from the dance halls of the 1900s to the discos of the seventies . . . from Glenn Miller to the Beatles . . . from Valentino to Newman . . . from corset to miniskirt . . . from beau to significant other.

Relive the moments . . . recapture the memories.

Watch for all the CENTURY OF AMERICAN ROMANCE titles in Harlequin American Romance. In one of the four American Romance books appearing each month, for the next ten months, we'll take you back to a decade of the twentieth century, where you'll relive the years and rekindle the romance of days gone by.

Don't miss a day of A CENTURY OF AMERICAN ROMANCE.

The women . . . the men . . . the passions . . .the memories . . .

Harlequin Superromance®

A powerful restaurant conglomerate that draws the best and brightest to its executive ranks. Now almost eighty years old, Vanessa Hamilton, the founder of Hamilton House, must choose a successor.
Who will it be?

Matt Logan: He's always been the company man, the quintessential team player. But tragedy in his daughter's life and a passionate love affair made him make some hard choices....

Paula Steele: Thoroughly accomplished, with a sharp mind, perfect breeding and looks to die for, Paula thrives on challenges and wants to have it all ...
but is this right for her?

Grady O'Connor: Working for Hamilton House was his salvation after Vietnam. The war had messed him up but good and had killed his storybook marriage. He's been given a second chance—only he doesn't know what the hell he's supposed to do with it....

Harlequin Superromance invites you to enjoy Barbara Kaye's dramatic and emotionally resonant miniseries about mature men and women making life-changing decisions. Don't miss:

- CHOICE OF A LIFETIME—a July 1990 release.
  - CHALLENGE OF A LIFETIME
    —a December 1990 release.
- CHANCE OF A LIFETIME—an April 1991 release.

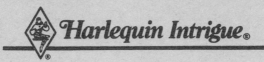

Nicole had a second chance...
to live.

One moment Nicole was standing in the deli's doorway, smiling at the handsome oceanographer. The next, she reached out to stop the gunman who'd jumped out of the rain-shrouded Manhattan day.

But when Nicole awoke, it was early morning August 30, a full week earlier. Had she been dreaming? Doubt grew stronger as the day unfolded—a day she remembered before it had even begun. Then she again met the oceanograher—David Germaine—and her world shifted on its axis.

David was her desire, her destiny, her only hope of averting disaster. Could this memorable stranger help her reverse fate? Meantime, dark forces gathered....

Don't miss this exciting Harlequin Intrigue coming this July wherever Harlequins are sold.... Watch for #142 *Déjà Vu* by Laura Pender!

HI-142-1

A BIG SISTER
can take her places

She likes that. Her Mom does too.

BIG BROTHERS/BIG SISTERS AND HARLEQUIN

Harlequin is proud to announce its official sponsorship of Big Brothers/Big Sisters of America. Look for this poster in your local Big Brothers/Big Sisters agency or call them to get one in your favorite bookstore. Love is all about sharing.

COMING SOON